MW00957963

Southern Bound

A MAX PORTER PARANORMAL MYSTERY

by Stuart Jaffe

Southern Bound is a work of fiction. Names, characters, places, and incidents either are the product of the author's imagination or are used fictitiously, and any resemblance to any persons, living or dead, business establishments, events, or locales is entirely coincidental.

SOUTHERN BOUND

All rights reserved.

Copyright © 2012 by Stuart Jaffe
    Cover art by Duncan Long

    ISBN 13: 978-1477633427
    ISBN 10: 1477633421

    First Edition: June, 2012
    Second Edition, May 2014

For Glory

Also by Stuart Jaffe

For more information visit www.stuartjaffe.com

Acknowledgments

No book is created by one person, and this is no exception. My sincere thanks goes out to Rod Hunter who made crucial contributions to the story; the wonderful people at the Z. Smith Reynolds Library at Wake Forest University; the dedicated people of Old Salem; Duncan Long for his stunning artwork; my good friend, Garrett; all of my family for their support; and my closest and dearest, Glory and Gabe. And of course, none of this is worth anything without you, the reader. Thank you.

Southern Bound

Chapter 1

MAX PORTER STOOD AT THE DOOR of his new office — old wood with a frosted-glass window; the 319 painted in gold and outlined in black. The keys jingled in his trembling right hand. His left held Sandra's hand tight. He wanted this job to go well for them. It had to.

Seven months without work had cleaned out the savings account Sandra's father started on their wedding day. They had nothing left. The endless job search during a recession had been gut-wrenching. So when an opportunity came along, even one that meant moving to the South, even one as weird as this one, Max grabbed it. Seeing Sandra's huge smile as he handed her the key made the decision feel right.

"You're sure it's okay for me to come in?" she asked.

"The note didn't say anything about you."

"I know, but it was so specific about a lot of things. Maybe we should check it again."

Max laughed. "Go inside. I've got the job."

With a girlish shrug, she kissed him quick and unlocked the door. The office dated back to the 1940s, and much of the original work remained — hardwood floors, two built-in bookcases with ornate but not obnoxious molding, a small bathroom on the opposite side, and three large windows giving view to the old Winston-Salem YMCA across the street (the word BOYS carved into the stone above one entrance, the word MEN above the other). Faux-lemon cleaners coated the air, and Max noticed the lack of dust anywhere.

He stepped closer to the bookshelves. His footsteps echoed around the high ceiling. He saw rows of reference materials — two German-English dictionaries, a full set of encyclopedias, a ten-volume local history, basic biology, geology, and physics textbooks, a few bits of fiction, and even some on divination.

"Strange," Max whispered, letting out a long breath he didn't know he had been holding.

"Got another note," Sandra said standing in front of an imposing oak desk with a heavy, leather desk chair and two less impressive guest chairs. He followed her gaze to the desk blotter where he saw a manila envelope with his name written in a fancy script bordering on calligraphy. Beneath his name, in bold block letters read — OPEN IN PRIVATE.

Sandra hugged Max long and tight. "Told you he didn't want me here."

"What makes you think my boss is a *he?*"

"Much too dictatorial for a woman."

Max thumbed the envelope's corner. His failure to deal with a dictatorial boss had led to his firing. *It was more than that,* he thought but buried those memories as fast as they threatened to emerge.

"You have your own job to get to, you know."

"Danishes and bread can wait."

"Honey, oh my, gee whiz, you should've told me you became the owner of a bakery. I can quit right now."

"Don't you dare," she laughed. "And don't worry. I'm going," she said with a wink. "Unless you want to play on the desk."

Chuckling, Max pointed to the door. "You're only

offering that 'cause you know I can't accept."

"You'll have to wait until tonight to find out."

A man standing in the doorway cleared his throat. He wore a tailored H. Huntsman suit and smelled clean like he had just stepped from a shower. Not a whisker stood on his face nor did a hair dare to stray from its assigned location. "You're early," he said.

Max recognized the voice right away. The same voice that had called to interview him for a job for which he had not applied. The same voice that had hired him and helped negotiate the move to North Carolina. The same voice that had set him up with a used car, a decent apartment, and a signing bonus to get them started. Mr. Modesto.

"We are early," Sandra said, extending her hand. "We were too excited to wait."

Mr. Modesto looked upon Sandra like an insect. "You were not to bring guests this morning."

"I was just leaving," she said, mouthing *Told you so* to Max and adding, "Have a great first day. Love you."

Sandra patted the door as she exited. He watched her move down the hall to the stairs on the end — her dark hair dancing on her shoulders, her not-too-thin *I'm a real woman* physique moving with enthusiasm. She made waking each morning worthwhile.

A hall door opened and an old lady with a coffee mug picked up her morning paper. She scowled at him. Modesto closed the door and said in his deep voice, "This building consists of apartments, some offices, and on the first floor, a small art gallery. Please keep in mind you have neighbors." With a disapproving glare, he added, "You've not opened the envelope?"

"It says 'Open In Private'."

"Then I'll wait in the hall," Modesto said and stepped out.

A little part of Max, a childish, naïve part, wanted to sprint down the hall, out the building, and head straight back to Michigan. He understood Michigan — Lansing, Alpena, Kalamazoo, it didn't matter what part of the state — cold, hard, practical with a side of cutting loose. This envelope had none of those qualities. It was a bizarre way to handle business.

A book clattered to the floor, and Max jumped in his seat, letting out a girlish screech. Then he laughed at himself — hard. Modesto probably thought him mad.

Careful, Max, the South just might make you nutty.

Max recomposed himself and opened the envelope. It read:

MR. PORTER —

WELCOME TO WINSTON-SALEM AND YOUR NEW OFFICE. IF YOU REQUIRE ANYTHING, DO NOT HESITATE TO CONTACT MR. MODESTO. YOUR FIRST TASK IS TO RESEARCH UNITAS FRATRUM. THE BOOKS PROVIDED HERE SHOULD SUFFICE BUT IF YOU REQUIRE ANY OTHERS, DO NOT HESITATE TO CONTACT MR. MODESTO. AT THE END OF EACH DAY, REPLACE EACH BOOK IN THE EXACT PLACE YOU FOUND IT. MAKE NO MARKS IN THE BOOKS. WITH THE EXCEPTION OF BASIC USAGE OF YOUR CHAIR, DO NOT MOVE ANY FURNITURE IN THIS OFFICE. DO NOT ADD OR REMOVE ANY FURNITURE IN THIS OFFICE. IF ANY LIGHT BULBS

NEED TO BE REPLACED OR ANY
OTHER SUPPLIES ARE REQUIRED, DO
NOT HANDLE IT YOURSELF. PLEASE
CONTACT MR. MODESTO INSTEAD.

No signature. No explanations.

He pulled open the top-right drawer and found a small ledge with three pens — nice pens, Monte Blanc. He picked one and then tried the drawer beneath. As he leaned down, he noticed some metal screwed into the underside of the desk. He had seen this type of thing before but only in old black-and-white movies. It was a gun tray meant for holding a small caliber weapon that would be pointed towards the door.

"Wild," he said.

In the bottom drawer, he found one plain, spiral notebook — the kind he preferred to work with. *Well, the boss does his homework,* he thought, smirking at his own use of the male pronoun. Sandra could turn him around on many things with just a few words.

Mr. Modesto returned with his eyes surveying the office (*checking that I haven't moved anything,* Max thought), and said, "I trust everything is clear and to your satisfaction."

As much as Mr. Modesto already pushed Max's desire to spew out sarcasm, he had to focus on keeping the job. Strange orders and a pompous manager should be the last of his concerns. "Um, just one thing," he said, hating the contrition in his voice.

"Oh?"

Gesturing to the empty desk, Max said, "No computer. I've got my own laptop. I can—"

"Our employer wishes for this room not to be altered. A technology such as that would severely alter the room."

"Perhaps our employer did not explain to you that

you're to help me out. It says so in this letter."

Mr. Modesto's face tightened. "The contents of that letter are marked 'private' and you should not be divulging them to me. As for my duties, I am well aware of what I am to do."

"Our employer wants some in-depth research done, and I'm assuming he wants it done in a timely manner. Without a computer, this task will be—"

"It is a short drive to the Wake Forest campus. You will find an excellent library there which will supplement any research requirements this room does not fulfill. Including a computer."

Max held his tongue for a moment and forced a pleasant face. "My apologies. I'm sure the University will be more than enough."

"I'll be checking in this office a few times each week. If you require anything for your research that does not violate my other orders, I'll be more than willing to help you. Also ..." Mr. Modesto's eyes narrowed on the floor as he walked toward the bookshelves. In one graceful motion, he swiped the book off the floor, snapped it shut and returned it to its rightful place. Without looking at Max, Mr. Modesto said, "Keep your focus on your research. These other matters are none of your concern. Good day." He walked out of the office, never once glancing back.

Max rubbed his forehead with his sleeve. A little sweat had broken out — he had to be careful. Mr. Modesto had been working for their boss a lot longer — Max had no leverage.

He could hear Sandra warning him to keep his cool, and she was right. In this economy, he had been more than lucky to land a good-paying job. Especially considering that right before the market crumbled, Sandra had just started out as a real estate agent in Michigan. She had a few contacts in the Southern real estate world, but upon moving, they all told her the same thing — find a different job. She did, at a bakery, but that didn't bring in enough on its own. Max needed to keep his job.

With a stretch, Max stood and checked out the bookshelves. He wasn't trying to be difficult. He simply couldn't stand when people purposefully did the wrong thing because they had the power to do so. Like Mr. Modesto and this job — they wanted him to do research. No problem. Let him do the research. Don't make up all these stupid rules to control him. No computer? Don't move the furniture? Come on.

To prove his point, Max lifted the edge of the desk and set it down an inch forward. He waited. "Nope," he said to the room. "Not struck by lightning."

From the corner of his eye, he saw something. Max jumped back and scanned the office. Empty.

With cautious motions, he turned his head toward the floor. There, curving under his desk, Max saw the edges of colored lines. Something had been drawn on the floor.

His hand tapped the edge of the desk, wanting to shift it just a tiny bit more, but his heart pounded a warning. "Aw, hell. In for a penny," he said, grabbed the desk and yanked it to the side.

A large circle had been painted in red and blue. Zodiac symbols marked compass points on the circle's inside edge. Two concentric circles were inside the largest one, and each also had symbols on the inside lines, but Max did not recognize them. Painted blood red, a jagged-toothed mouth occupied the center — one of four serpent heads attached to the same body.

Cocking his head to the side, he read the words *cruor* and *teneo*. They meant nothing to him but sent shivers straight through to his hands.

He slid the desk back in place, covering the circle, and glanced at it from several angles. It appeared to be in the same spot. He checked from his desk chair — only with a flashlight would he have ever found the circle.

Research, he thought with relief. Get out of the office. Get fresh air. Do what he had been hired to do. Forget about this other nonsense.

Max gathered his things and headed out. As he walked by the bookshelf, his eyes caught the book that kept falling out. Its cracked spine read — WITCHCRAFT IN WINSTON-SALEM, VOL 7, 1935-1950.

"Holy crap," he whispered and hurried his steps.

Chapter 2

MAX LOVED THE WAY the Z. Smith Reynolds Library at Wake Forest University really was two separate structures — the former alleyway had been enclosed long ago to form an exquisite reading space full of light and air. Like any good library, Wake's was a labyrinth of floors and nooks and dusty corners each promising to hold great discoveries for anybody bold enough to explore. For Max, if he wanted to be honest with himself, he would admit that he loved doing research, and he loved being in this quiet, solitary sanctuary. Teaching had its joys, but the students always made him feel unfulfilled.

After several minutes on the library computers, Max had a few call numbers to check out. Later, he could use what he learned to validate the accuracy of any websites claiming to have information. This approach took more effort than just using Google, but since he was being paid for quality work, he figured it was worth it. Which meant that for now, books were the place to start.

He climbed a narrow staircase to the seventh floor. Most of the lights were off and each row of stacks had a separate switch. In the quiet, he worked his way through until he matched the call numbers, popped on the light, and started searching through the old titles.

Research was a treasure hunt, and as the familiar

sensations of discovery flooded into him, he began talking to the texts — a habit that Sandra found amusing, annoying, and sometimes cute. "You look promising," he muttered to a reddish-brown book.

Hours passed with Max sitting in a cubicle, his head stuck between book covers. His hand ached from taking notes (he made a mental note to bring his laptop next time), but a picture of Winston-Salem's early years had formed, one that struck him as both daring and desperate.

In the 15th Century, in Moravia, a Czech named Jan Hus preached about a church based on moral purity and conduct rather than doctrine and consistency. His disciples, the Brethren, called the new church *Unitas Fratrum,* and by 1467, they seceded from the Church of Rome.

Max predicted the backlash would not be pretty. Nobody seceded from the Church without repercussions — often violent repercussions. For the Brethren, he read on, persecution and dispersal rained upon them for hundreds of years.

"Told ya," Max said.

A door squeaked open. Max glanced around, heard a few footsteps, and settled back to his book.

In the 17th Century, the Brethren hanging on in Germany found a safe haven in Count Nicholas Ludwig von Zinzendorf. He provided them his Saxony estate, an arrangement that lasted many years. In 1722, the Moravians (as they were becoming known) created the Renewed Unitas Fratrum ("Such originality," Max said) with Zinzendorf as their leader. Shortly after, they began missionary work.

Max jotted down these key dates. He imagined Zinzendorf angered a lot of Brethren. Many would have accused him of purchasing his leadership role. Others, well, religious politics always had been as bloody as the secular variety.

Max heard a single beep and whispering. He swore he heard his name. He glanced around, but the stacks and the darkened floor hid just about everything. Again, he heard the whispering followed by the beep.

"Now," he said, trying to bury the nervousness growing inside, "America has to come into the picture."

Seeking religious freedom, word of America worked its way to the Moravians. In 1741, after a failed attempt to settle in Georgia, they founded the town of Bethlehem in Pennsylvania. A decade later, they bought land in North Carolina and settled Bethabara. Later growth led to Bethania, and in 1765, construction of Salem began.

Another beep.

"Hello?" Max said, his voice sounding unnaturally loud in the library's quiet.

Several stacks down, a figure darted into the main aisle. Max jumped from his chair to peek down the aisle just in time to see the fire door closing. His skin prickled.

He shook off the feeling, unwilling to give it much credence. After all, if he voiced the idea that somebody had been watching him, perhaps following him, perhaps checking up on him — he didn't want to consider what that implied.

By noon, Max was finished with his initial survey. He met Sandra at a little diner and was surprised at her excitement.

She bit into her cheeseburger with a strong appetite. "This has been a great day," she said. Max gnawed on a fry and quivered out a grin. "Everybody's been so nice."

"Nice?" Max said. *The word* creepy *described things far better.*

"I mean it. We have this reputation in the North of being harsh and cold and full of bite. I never felt it I guess because I lived there my whole life. But now, meeting these people down here — it's weird. Every single person here is nice."

"Real nice," Max said, thinking of the stranger in the library. In Michigan, he didn't have these kinds of problems. And they said the economy was picking up back there. Something would have come his way. Or he'd have done something online. Lots of people telecommute nowadays. This whole job smelled illegal anyway — but he had known that from the start.

Sandra continued, "I called to set up DSL today and when the lady found out we'd just moved in, she gave me the warmest welcome. Up North it's all, 'What do you want?' as if you're imposing on their time to sit on their asses and do nothing. Here, I don't know, I guess I expected banjo-pickers at the gas station ready to string us up if we looked at them wrong."

"It's definitely not like back home."

"And did you notice all the Japanese restaurants? There's also some Indian places and even Greek. We never had that. They're more cultured than we've ever been."

Max looked at Sandra's beaming face and his stomach dropped. First day of work, less than a week living here, and she already had fallen for the place. And the money — they would never get back on their feet without real money coming in like this.

She must have picked up something in his body language, she could always read him well, because she stopped talking, clasped his hands, and said, "Did something go wrong at work?"

Max sniffled and shook his head. "Mr. Modesto. I don't care for him."

"Well, no job is perfect, honey."

"I know."

"And we need this money. We still owe the credit card company —"

"I know," he said with more force than he intended.

They grew silent, and Max thought about the tension their silences had acquired. There was a time when he would bring her a single rose every day. She would see it, smile, and say nothing — those were the silences he craved. He leaned closer and said, "Hey, hon, guess what? I know my boss is a man."

"I told you that," she said with less bite and more play.

"When I was talking with Modesto, I referred to the boss as 'he' and the guy didn't say a word. Didn't even flinch."

"You're quite the detective."

"I try," Max said, a genuine smile opening up.

Sandra took his hands again. "I want you to help me make this work. This is our best opportunity."

"I will."

"And we can't afford not to take it."

"I know."

"So please, honey, deal with whatever nastiness this Modesto ass sends your way. Please."

He looked at those brown eyes and his heart lurched. "Okay," he said. "I'll try."

"Promise?"

"I promise."

"Then you are definitely getting lucky tonight."

Max burst into laughter and that sent Sandra into her own fit of giggles.

When he returned to his office, he received a surprise. Behind his desk, admiring the woodwork, sat a well-groomed man in his thirties, dressed in an old-style suit. He did not appear embarrassed at being caught messing with the desk nor did he even acknowledge Max's entrance.

Max cleared his throat. The man startled at the noise, then looked at Max with a different sense of surprise as if amazed Max could produce such a sound. Finally, he stood (a rather tall, strong body) and said, "You the boss here?"

"Max Porter. Pleased to meet you," he said offering his hand.

The man ignored Max's hand but said, "Name's Drummond. Marshall Drummond."

"Well, what can I do for you?" Max said as he sat in his chair, forcing Drummond toward the guest side of the desk.

"Other way around, friend. I'm going to help you."

"You are?"

"Maybe. After you do something for me."

"Make up your mind," Max said, writing a mental note to ask Modesto for some kind of security.

"What I mean is ..." Drummond said, his focus drifting to the bookshelf.

"Mr. Drummond?"

"The world is much stranger than I ever thought."

Max shifted in his chair. "If I can help you with something, please tell me. Otherwise, I've got a lot to do and I'm going to have to ask you to leave."

Drummond's eyes snapped onto Max with a fierceness that dried Max's throat. "Are you?"

"Yes."

"I'm waiting."

"Excuse me."

"You said you'd have to ask me to leave. Go ahead. Ask."

"Um ... will you please leave?"

"No."

Drummond sat in the left guest chair, leaned back, and rested his feet on the desk. Max sighed as he rose to his feet. "Look, I'm not interested in stupid power games. Leave or I'll call the police."

"You need to listen up. I know a heck of a lot more about things around here than you. And I'm willing to help you out because right now, our interests are pretty much the same. After all, don't you want to know who's pulling your strings? So, sit." Drummond waited. Max held still a moment, his brain tumbling to catch up on how fast the tone of this meeting had altered. He sat. "Good."

"What do you know about my boss?"

Drummond chuckled. "Stan Bowman."

"That's his name?"

"No. That's the name I want you to find out about. I want to know what happened to that bastard. You find that out, and I'll tell you all about this office, that book that keeps falling out, and the witch's spell under your desk."

Max's stomach churned hard. "Witch's spell?"

"Stan Bowman. Research him and I'll tell you."

With a shaking hand, Max pulled out a pencil and wrote down the name *Stan Bowman*. "O-Okay," he said, "What else?"

"Don't do this from here. Got it?"

"Yes."

"I'll meet you tomorrow."

"Okay."

"And don't say a word to Modesto about me, Bowman, or this meeting. You so much as hint about it, you'll find out how bad things can get."

Chapter 3

MAX TRIED TO KEEP SILENT around his wife that night. He told himself that he wanted to find out all about Stan Bowman, find out about Drummond, find out anything, any concrete answer, before he spoke with Sandra. Otherwise, she would be full of questions and he would be full of idiotic silence. She would worry and regret relocating. She would find some way to blame herself.

But as he searched and googled and combed through the quieter corners of the internet, as he learned more about Stan Bowman and what became of the man, Max knew he had to release the mounting pressure within. He had to tell her so he could blot out the pictures in his mind. He had to tell her so he could sleep. Not all of it — he couldn't be so cruel, but some ... yeah, he had to tell her about that sick monster.

Around nine, they settled in for a late meal of fried rice, lo mein, and some wine, and he started. "I met this man, Drummond," he said, keeping his eyes on his food. "He had me look into this horrible story about Stan Bowman."

"What?" Sandra said, her voice snapping hard as her face twisted into a *you've-got-to-be-joking* smile.

"It's just a little side trip, that's all. And he said he could give me information about —"

"Stop it. Right now. I mean it. You can't go screw this

up for us."

"Honey, I'm not going to —"

"You have a job. One that pays you well. And you know if they find out you're working for somebody else on their dollar, they'll fire you." All the harshness fled Sandra as she crossed her arms and fought her tears. "We can't afford that. We'll lose everything."

"I'm not getting fired."

"You said that in Michigan," Sandra said, her mouth a tight line.

Max downed his glass of wine and then breathed deep. "I thought that was all behind us. You said you forgave me. We're supposed to be building a new life down here. Now I'm trying my best. You like it here, right? The people are nice and all, right?"

Sandra nodded.

"Okay. Then allow me a little room to find where I fit in. I won't lose my job. I'm doing this research at home on my own time. I never signed anything, never agreed to anything that says I can't do this thing at home. Besides, if they try to fire me for the way I use my personal time, we'll sue them for millions, and then all our money troubles will be gone."

Sandra let out a relieved shudder. "I'm not happy about it."

"I see that."

"But okay."

Max kissed her hand. "I love you."

"You piss me off lots, but I love you, too."

Refilling their glasses, Max said, "So, do you want to hear about Stan Bowman?"

"No, but you'll tell me anyway."

They both laughed a bit too hard — the wine contributing as much as the tension. "Okay," Max said, and as he summoned the images and story in his head, his face hardened. Sandra must have seen the change in his demeanor because her laughter died and her concern returned.

"During World War II," Max began, "Winston-Salem gave three-hundred-and-one men to the fight. Stan Bowman lucked out, though. He only got shot in the leg. Before he left, he was a decent enough man, I guess. Helped out with the scouts and stuff like that. I don't know for sure, of course. Online info isn't that trustworthy. Plus, there's only so much you can get from newspapers and police statements."

"Police? That doesn't sound good."

"It isn't. He had a girlfriend, but she left while he was in Africa. By the time he returned to the States, she had married and had a kid. But he met a new gal and married her — Annabelle Grier. She told the police that Stan suffered terrible nightmares, waking up drenched in cold sweat, that kind of thing."

"Sounds like Post Traumatic Stress."

Max nodded. "Everything probably would've just settled into your typical nuclear-family, fake-happiness thing, been just fine — except the POWs arrived."

"POWs?"

"R. J. Reynolds just about owned all of Winston-Salem. His tobacco company employed a huge percentage of the city. Heck, he built Wake Forest University."

"Well, his money did."

"You know what I mean. Anyway, at the time, he was providing the cigarettes for the soldiers. Demand was huge, and he started having trouble keeping up production. So, he managed to get a deal with the government to ship over German POWs and put them to work in his factories."

"Are you serious?"

"It's all true. Two hundred and fifty soldiers came, all of them from Rommel's Afrika Korps."

"And Stan served in Africa."

"Right."

"Oh, that can't be good," Sandra said, and Max saw that she had become intrigued. He had to admit it — despite his fears, he was intrigued, too. He sipped his wine, making her wait a moment before he continued.

"About a month after the Germans arrived, Stan goes missing. Annabelle contacts the police, says she hasn't seen Stan in two days, but apparently, they don't give her much credence. Stan had been known as a heavy drinker, so the police figured he'd gone on a binge and would turn up sooner or later. Of course, Stan wasn't drinking."

"Of course."

"One by one in turn, seven POWs go missing. Each one abducted from the factory floor," Max said, pausing to let his words sink deep inside.

"Wait," Sandra said a moment later. "How's that possible? I mean, these are POWs. There had to be guards all around. I know our government can do some stupid things, but they wouldn't let a bunch of German soldiers loose in America. Would they?"

"No, honey, there were plenty of guards. Best anybody figured out was that the abductions took place during bathroom breaks. But here's where it gets interesting. In each case, the prisoner was found several days later, gibbering like a madman, completely nuts. Only one thing they said made any sense — each one mentions the name Stan Bowman. The police go on a manhunt, but nobody ever finds Stan. A private detective, however, does locate this little apartment-type room in an old warehouse. The place must have reeked of tobacco. Inside, they find Stan's workplace. He'd been torturing these men, but not just physically. He messed with their heads. Hours and hours of slow, mind-boggling torture."

Sandra stood to clear the table. "And they never found him?"

"He disappeared."

She placed a hand on her hip. "You can't possibly be serious about following this."

"Why not? It's fascinating."

"Hon, you're talking about crazy people doing crazy things over seventy years ago. Nothing good could ever come from digging this up."

"Come with me," Max said, getting up. "I want to show you one of the crime photos. Relax, it's not bloody. I just want you to see something that'll make it clearer to you."

With a reluctant stretch, Sandra followed. The bedroom of their apartment doubled as an office for Max, so she settled on the bed while he scooted into the small desk chair in the corner. He pulled up the photo on his laptop and angled it for her to see.

The black-and-white photo depicted a stool in the middle of an unfinished room. Two buckets had been placed next to the stool, one clearly filled with a dark substance. Gruesome pictures of women and children being shot or tortured had been nailed to some of the wall studs. Straight in front of the stool, Stan had mounted a film screen. Two detectives were shown in the photo — both looked queasy.

"Stan forced his victims to stay awake the whole time, or I suppose, as long as Stan could handle it himself. Nobody ever found what film he showed them but based on the wall pictures, I'm guessing it ain't a Disney classic."

"Okay, now I'm thinking this Stan guy is super nuts. Why is this going to convince me you should get involved?"

"Because," Max said pointing to the detective standing

near the stool, "this man here is the spitting image of Drummond. Very strong family resemblance."

"It's still a bunch of crazy people."

"You're missing the point, honey. Drummond is interested in this because of a family matter. This detective had to have been some close relation. The Stan Bowman crazy part of all this is secondary. This guy is just looking for a lost relative."

Sandra frowned. "You really believe that?"

"If that's all it is, then I might be able to help him out, help him find his family. I do that, and I'm sure he'll pay well. We need all we can get." Before Sandra could speak, Max put out his hand. "If it's something more, I'll let it go. Don't worry. I'm not getting fired."

Sandra crossed her arms but didn't protest further. Max smiled.

The next day, Max bolted down his breakfast and rushed to the office. To his pleasure, he found Drummond waiting for him.

"I take it you found some things," Drummond said.

Max circled his desk, pulled out a hard copy of the photo, and tossed it down. "I'd say I'm getting somewhere."

Drummond looked at the photo and grimaced. "Boy, I haven't seen this in a long time."

"So, what's the relation?"

"I can still smell the place."

"Your grandfather?"

"What?"

"Huh?"

Max sat on the edge of his chair, his knee bumping the gun tray screwed into the desk's underside. "You've been to this place?" he asked.

"You think this is my grandfather? You did look closely at this picture, right? I'm right there."

"Mr. Drummond, that picture is seventy years old."

"I know. Last one of me ever taken. Two days later I wound up dead. Shot right here in my office."

"Your office?"

"Are you pretending to be this lost?"

"No," Max said, his face locked in total confusion.

"Let me lay it down for you. In the 1940s, I was a private investigator. The police called in for my help on the Bowman case, and then I was murdered. Pretty clear now?"

"So ... you're ... dead?"

"Yup, I'm dead."

Chapter 4

MAX LET OUT A NERVOUS LAUGH as he stood and worked his way from the desk. His chest tightened and his face heated up. Now he understood why rich people had panic rooms or emergency buttons installed.

"You don't believe me," Drummond said.

"Take it easy. Just stay calm."

"I'm completely calm. You're the one whose voice is rising. I'm sorry to rattle you, but this is the way it is."

Max wanted to break for the door, but he would have to pass right by Drummond. He glanced out the window. Three stories high — too far for any kind of escape.

"Look," Drummond said, straightening his blazer as he stood. "Let me prove to you that I'm dead. Then, if you can't handle it, I'll just go away. Okay? That sound fair?"

Max nodded, his mind otherwise blank.

"Good," Drummond said and stepped forward until he stood in the middle of the desk, the top slicing right through his body.

Max let out a tight-lipped screech. With his eyes locked on the bizarre sight, blood drained from his head, paling his skin and making him light-headed.

"Don't pass out on me," Drummond said. "I hated it when women did that, I'm really going to be angry if you do it. Just take some deep breaths and sit down."

Following instructions, Max breathed deep and eased down to the floor. The room swirled around him as sweat beaded on his forehead. For a second, he thought he was nine and visiting the Fun House for the first time. He motioned for Drummond to step away, and Drummond complied.

With a smile from one side of his mouth, Drummond said, "You're going to be fine, kiddo. I see color coming back to your face. Have a drink. That'll do the trick."

"I-I don't have anything."

"Lucky for you this is Marshall Drummond's old office. Fourth book from the right, bottom shelf — my gift to you."

Despite his shaking hands, Max crawled to the bookshelf and found a copy of *Beyond This Horizon* by Anson MacDonald. Inside the hollowed out book, he found a silver flask. He glanced at Drummond, received a knowing nod, and grabbed the flask. The whiskey it contained slipped down Max's throat, warming his body, and calming his nerves.

Without waiting for Max to settle back, Drummond said, "Good. Now that that's done, let's talk about Stan Bowman."

"B-But you're a ghost."

Like a weary school teacher, Drummond said, "We've covered this already. I'm a ghost and you're in my office. You're going to help me and I will help you."

"But you're *a ghost*."

"Are we going to have a problem?"

Max's gut dropped a bit, but he managed to shake his head. "You need to answer some questions first."

"My, aren't we bold with well-aged whiskey?"

Perhaps a little whiskey had helped. It certainly relaxed him enough to see that this thing — this ghost — before him could not be denied. It was real. Ghosts were real. Marshall Drummond, dead since the forties, stood in Max's office.

And he hadn't tried to kill Max. Or even scare him. Drummond was asking for his help. With his brain wrapping around this idea, Max felt much better.

With a slight grunt, Max got to his feet and paced the room. The movement got his circulation running again, and he could feel his thinking process kicking in. "For starters, why did you wait until now to show yourself? I've been here for awhile."

"I couldn't. All I could do was drop that book."

"That was you?"

"You know any other dead people?"

"Okay," Max said, his pacing getting faster. "Why couldn't you show yourself?"

Drummond nodded towards the floor. "That symbol is a curse that was put on me."

"A curse?"

"A witchcraft sort of thing. I'd been investigating the Stan Bowman case when it happened. They attacked me with four guys, and the next thing I know, I'm spread on the floor, bleeding slowly all over, and they've drawn this whole mess here. When I finally died, I was stuck."

"Stuck?"

"I can't leave. Not with that thing here. The curse ties me to this office. And as long as everything in here is in the exact place it was when they finished the curse, I can't even show myself. If I move something, like the books, it doesn't matter. I've tried. It only works if a living person does it, and whatever was moved has to stay moved for quite awhile. Otherwise, I'm locked away."

"But I see you now."

"That's right. You moved the desk."

"I put it back," Max said, his eyes darting to the desk's feet. Looking far closer than ever before, he saw a sliver of a circle marking where the desk had been for many years. "Modesto," he said.

"Yeah, I'm pretty sure he noticed," Drummond said.

"Wait a second. Modesto knows about the desk, and I was even given orders not to move the desk. Are you telling me my employer did this to you?"

"What do you know — you're not so slow after all."

Max rubbed his face. "I think I need another drink."

"We got a lot of work ahead, so take all the liquid courage you need."

"No, no, no. I'm not getting into this any worse. No. I'll quit the job. Sandra and I, we'll go back to Michigan. The heck with this."

"Sorry, pal. Maybe last week you could've gotten away with it. I doubt it, but you could've tried. Now that you've seen me, now that Modesto knows you moved the desk, Hull's not going to let you go."

"Hull?" Max asked. "Is that my employer's name?"

Drummond pulled back. "You went to work for somebody you never met, and you don't even know his name? Are you insane?"

"I'm not the one ended up a cursed-ghost, so you better hold off on all the judging."

"Whatever."

"You speak like somebody from today? I thought you died in the forties."

"Back to doubting me, huh? I did die in the forties, kiddo, and I've been stuck here ever since. I've seen generations come through these doors and I've *listened* to them. I remember in the sixties, this couple squatted here for awhile. Used to screw on my desk everyday when they weren't too stoned to do it. I got so sick of the word *groovy* I wanted to die — if I wasn't already dead."

Despite all the fear and trepidation surging through Max, he chuckled. "Okay, so who's Hull?"

"William Hull, and I don't know much about him other than what everybody knows — very rich, very powerful, very private family. I was just turning my focus onto him when this happened to me."

"You think he did this to you?"

"I'm sure of it. This is his building."

"So, he finds out you're interested in him in connection with Stan Bowman and he kills you?"

"Strikes hard and fast. He's a dangerous man, that much should be obvious, and that means you are in a dangerous situation."

Max grabbed the flask and swung back a little more whiskey. "What was the connection to Bowman?"

"I don't know," Drummond said. "His company owned the warehouse where Stan took the POWs. That was it. I wanted to talk to him as a matter of routine but his people stonewalled me. That got me heated up. I started looking into court records, newspapers, anything I could find his name on. It all turned up empty, but I must've been getting close to something because here I am."

"Here you are," Max said, his brain finally putting pieces together. "Why, though? Why do this whole curse thing to you? Why not just kill you and get rid of the body?"

"You figure that one out, and we'll both be a lot happier."

Max grew quiet for a moment as he let all the things he had seen and heard settle inside him. In a calm tone that frightened him more than his anger ever had, he said, "He's going to come after me, isn't he?"

"Hull? Maybe. He might play this one a little different. In my case, he was trying to shut me up. For you, though, he hired you. He wants you looking into some things, right?"

"History of the area. That's all."

"As long as he doesn't know that we've talked, you should be able to stay alive long enough."

"For what?"

"To solve the Stan Bowman case."

"No way. No. Not going to happen."

"You don't have a choice, unless you want Sandra to be a widow. Or worse, they might go after her. Threaten you through her. I've seen much less men do much worse things."

Max blotted away the image of Modesto beating Sandra and focused on Drummond. For the moment, at least, Drummond made sense. What other choice did Max have? Of course, Drummond could be lying, but Max would have to figure that part out later. Whatever the truth, Max knew he stood at the foot of a mountain range of old pain, deceit, and treachery. He just prayed he'd find a way to climb to safety.

"Okay," he said, clearing away all the nagging words his conscience wanted to weigh on him, "where do we start?"

Chapter 5

BEFORE DRUMMOND COULD ANSWER, the office door opened and Mr. Modesto walked in. He nodded at Max, clearly unable to see Drummond, and sat in a guest chair.

"You and I are to have lunch," he said, disdain dripping from every word.

Max tried to look at the desk, to keep his eyes off Drummond, but he caught sight of the ghost disappearing into the bookcase. "It's a bit early for lunch," he managed to say while staring at the books.

Modesto stood, straightening his suit, and stepped between Max and where Drummond had been. "There is no need for rudeness. You and I are to have lunch this afternoon."

"I've got a lot of work to do. Instead, can we —"

"What makes you think our employer is any less specific with me in his instructions? Now, please acknowledge that you understand what I've said, so I know you will meet me."

"Okay, sure."

"Twelve-thirty."

"I'll be working on —"

"I don't really care."

When Modesto left, Max slumped into the desk chair and let out a long sigh. This was how he had lost his job in

Michigan — an early morning request to join the boss's assistant to lunch. False accusations came with that lunch. Before the entrees hit the table, his job had disappeared.

He should call Sandra. She would ease his mind. She knew what to say. But if he called her, she would also know that something else had happened, and he wasn't ready to explain about ghosts. Besides, there was no reason to think he had lost this job. He had moved the table, true. But could they really know that?

"Not unless they're bugging the office," Max chuckled. His eyes darted to the dark corners of the room. No, he refused to let paranoia attack. He had no control over this lunch, so best to just go to the library and get some work done. Whatever happens after that would happen regardless.

At 12:30 exactly, Mr. Modesto arrived and brought Max to the Village Tavern — a small restaurant adjacent to the university campus. Max loved the place the instant he stepped inside. It reminded him of visits to New York City — the dark, cramped restaurant that utilized every last inch of space, the jostle of people all grumpy with hunger, the clatter from the busy kitchen underscoring the delightful aromas drifting throughout. When they had money again, Max wanted to bring Sandra here to celebrate.

After they were seated, Mr. Modesto folded his hands on the table and said, "Tell me everything you've learned."

Max frowned. "I'm confused. I assumed I would be writing a report for our employer," he said, fully conscious that he had just used the phrase Modesto always applied to their boss.

"You will write a report, too. However, our employer desires a faster reply at the moment. So, tell me what you will eventually write down."

"Okay," Max said, holding back a sarcastic — *you asked for it.*

Halfway through their filet mignons, Max entered into the work he had explored in the last few days — the Moravian congregational government. "It's fascinating stuff," he said. "They divided their government into three branches just like America would do shortly afterward, but these branches acted very differently." Modesto appeared to pay attention in a polite manner but showed no surprise as Max explained the system. "The first branch was the Elders Conference. They dealt with the spiritual affairs of the congregation and ensured that all the various officials worked well together. The Congregation Council handled broader issues that affected the long-term — like an overseer. And last was the Aufesher Collegium which dealt with secular matters such as town administration."

"And this system worked?" Modesto asked, but something in his voice told Max he could care less. Max didn't mind, though. He'd babble for a week if it kept his mind off of ghosts.

"Well, it worked for them. They used their three-branch government to regulate all aspects of life so nobody would profit at somebody else's expense. They sought harmony for everybody."

"But it didn't always work that way, did it?"

"Of course not."

"And do you have any examples of this not working?"

Max took a bite of his steak to force a pause. Even as he discussed Winston-Salem's history with more enthusiasm than he realized he had for the subject, he found Modesto's attitude disturbing. Perhaps that's what the man wanted — he clearly did not like Max. Yet something else gnawed at Max.

"Surely you've come across at least one example?" Modesto said. "Our employer would be unhappy if your research was so superficial."

"I have examples."

Modesto ordered a cup of coffee and said, "I'm waiting. Just one example, please."

Like a bull let out of the shoot, Max barreled into a verbal assault. "In 1829, there's a man with the ironic name of Thomas Christman who decides to become a Baptist. He takes his son with him in this move away from the Moravian beliefs. Christman is ordered to leave town, but he refuses. This is considered a spiritual problem, so the Elders Council is called. They decide not to evict the man — they don't want to go through the North Carolina legal system. Instead, they buy the house from under Christman. He can still live there, but he owns nothing and has nothing for his son to inherit. They've effectively removed him from their world, though he still occupies its space."

"I see."

"You don't. It's not how strict, vengeful, or even creative these people can be, but rather how patient. They wanted a man who had betrayed their beliefs to be driven from their town, and they were willing to wait a lifetime in order for it to occur. Compare that to the Christians or the Muslims — two groups of many that are prone to act now in order to achieve their goals as soon as possible. The kind of patience displayed here is an amazing quality of the Moravians."

Modesto let out a sly grin. "You seem to be very excited about our little city in the South."

Not sure how to take the comment, Max sat back and spread his hands. "If I can't get interested, I wouldn't do a very good job at the research, would I?"

"That is beyond my expertise. Excuse me a moment," Modesto said as he stood. He placed his briefcase on his chair and inched by a waiter as he walked toward the restrooms.

Max looked at the briefcase and wondered at the point of this display. Was Modesto testing Max's trustworthiness? Was this an order from the boss or just a game from a jealous employee? And Modesto was jealous, Max had no doubt. The condescension oozing from Modesto's words could not be mistaken. Somehow he felt threatened by Max's presence. In fact, this entire lunch may not have been ordered by the boss.

Peeking over his shoulder, Max checked to see that Modesto was not heading back. Could this be some sort of probe into his work by Modesto? Max envisioned the arrogant prick groveling at the boss's feet, presenting Max's information as if it were his own.

As he considered this possibility, Max noticed the tip of a paper poking from the front sleeve of the briefcase like a teasing leg-shot on the cover of an old girlie mag. Checking once more that Modesto was not on his way back, Max leaned closer and made out a logo — the letter H in a blockish style, colored blue, with a white rectangle on the right leg as if it were a door or window.

When Modesto returned, he said, "I just spoke with our employer. He's pleased with your work."

"Good," Max said, and then part of what bothered him finally discovered its form. "Everything I've told you today was not difficult information to find. Rather basic, actually. Why would our employer want —"

"Our employer recognizes that you need a little time to catch up on the foundation before you can do the more serious studies. After all, you're still talking about Moravians. You haven't even begun to look into the Reynolds family which made this city noteworthy. So, your immediate job is to catch up. Our employer does not want to waste more than another week, if even that. I've hired an assistant for you to help you along. We particularly don't want you bogged down with the busy work of the reports."

"An assistant?"

"Yes," Modesto said as he readied to leave. "Once you're ready, the real work can begin. We'll be researching various land deals. I must go now. I'll be in touch next week."

As Modesto walked away, Max was surprised his thoughts were not of land deals, the blue H, or even Modesto. Instead, Max thought only of two names — Marshall Drummond and Stan Bowman.

Chapter 6

"I MUST BE CRAZY," Max said to his empty car as he drove toward the campus. "No, no. They say if you can think that might be the case, then it's not. Crazy people think they're perfectly normal. Then again, I'm talking to myself in a car, so what does that say for me?"

When his cell phone rang, Max answered it without looking at the name. His mother's voice screeched in his ear. "Max, I've been so worried about you. I've been trying to get you for days."

"Hi, Mom."

"You eating all right?"

"I'm fine, Mom. The move went fine, Sandra's fine, and we're just busy getting settled in."

"Oh, that's wonderful. Listen, I sent you a housewarming gift. Did you get it?"

"Yes, thank you," Max said, trying to blot out any memory of the ugliest ashtray ever made in the seventies — something she had lying around her attic.

"I'm glad it arrived. You never know with the mail. And since I didn't get a thank you note, I wasn't sure."

"Like I said, it's been busy."

He could hear his mother working herself into a nitpicking froth. "Well, I have to say that it doesn't take that long to write a thank you note, and it's very important. I know I taught you better than that. Now, I'm not joking. People will look down upon you in your life if you fail at the little things. It's that important, and it's a mark of a civilized person. For me, it's okay, it doesn't matter, you understand. You forget me, I don't mind. You're my son. I know you love me. But other people, they need to be properly thanked."

"Yes, Mom. I'm very sorry. I'll try to be better," Max said, not paying attention to his words as he took the Wake exit. By the time he found a parking spot (and hoped he'd avoid a ticket for using the student lot), his mother had wound down and said her good-byes. As annoying as she could be, though, Max wanted to thank her this time. By distracting him from all that had occurred that morning, she had managed to untangle his thoughts enough for him to function.

He still shuddered at the idea that a real ghost haunted his office, but he no longer feared the thing — especially since Drummond needed his help. His own situation bothered him far greater, yet even that no longer rattled him like earlier. Now, he started to see that Stan, Annabelle, Hull, and Drummond all were just the dots he had to connect. If he could do that, then perhaps he had nothing to worry about. Besides, as odd as his employer had been, it was only Drummond saying that Max was in danger.

A ghost might say anything to be freed from a curse. And what, exactly, did he do to deserve a curse?

By the time Max entered the now-familiar library lobby, his curiosity had risen above the tide line of his fear. No matter what else, Max agreed with one thing Drummond had said — he needed to find Annabelle Bowman.

After an hour had passed, Max admitted that all his research that day on Moravian history did nothing to help him find Annabelle Bowman. It did, however, help Max avoid thinking about ghosts and dangerous bosses. *Don't slow down. Keep pushing ahead.* As long as he kept moving forward, logic and common sense would prevail. He hoped.

Leafing through a pictorial history of Winston-Salem as he climbed a stairwell, Max jolted at the sound of his cell phone ringing. A glance at the phone's face — Sandra. Max sat on the stairs (cell phone reception only happened in the library's stairwells) with the book on his lap and answered.

Sandra's day had not fared any better than Max's. She launched into a detailed account of being rear-ended by "some jerk in a jaguar who insisted on pulling over and getting an official police report even though all I got was a scratch on the bumper." She ended up late to work and had to deal with a lecture from Mrs. McCarthy, the owner, that ended with a reminder, "There's lots of good people looking for work right now. People who know how to be on time."

Max listened and did not interrupt. The more she spoke, the less he wanted to say. What could he tell her? That a ghost hired him on the side and promised him that his new employer, the one that would save them financially, was somehow associated with the spawn of evil, Stan Bowman? But he didn't want to lie to her either.

When she finished, still huffing at unspoken thoughts, the dreaded question came out. "So, what happened with Drummond?"

Turning the page in his book, Max saw a picture of a large building on fire in the middle of a field while numerous, well-dressed people stood at a distance and watched. The caption explained that on November 24, 1892 the Zinzendorf Hotel (named after the beloved former leader) tragically burned to the ground in about two hours. Max looked at the billowing smoke and wondered if he had started his own tragic fire.

"Honey?" Sandra said.

"I'm here. Things have gotten a little bit more complicated, but don't worry."

"Just tell Drummond —"

"Don't do that."

"Do what?"

"Try to solve my problems and tell me what to do. I've got it all being taken care of. And I can decide for my own career if I want to do a little work for Drummond or not. I promise you I won't be fired from my job. Okay?"

"I guess I'm just a little worried that —"

"We're not in Michigan anymore."

"I know," Sandra said. With forced levity, she changed the subject, and as she chattered on, Max flipped through a few more pages.

"It can't be," he said, staring at a picture from the 1980s. He read the caption twice.

"What did you say?"

"She might still be here."

"Who?"

"Annabelle. I've got to go. I'll see you tonight," Max said, cutting the connection without any further good-bye.

He went to his cubicle, gathered his things, and rushed to the microtext room. With the aid of a librarian, he found several spools containing all issues of the local paper, The Winston-Salem Journal, for the year 1989. In a short time, he found the story he had sought, and the photos of several Winston-Salem residents, including an older lady attempting to hide behind harsh-looking men — but her spry eyes gave her away. Annabelle Bowman. A quick search online gave him the address.

As he drove to the South Side home, Max considered calling Drummond. Two thoughts stopped him. First, he saw no reason he should feel obligated to make reports.

Second, and far more important, Drummond was dead. How would a ghost answer the phone?

The house appeared to be nothing special. A beaten Chevy with a layer of dust resided in the driveway and leaves dotted the walk. Fall would arrive soon, but for the moment, the warm air felt just right. As Max waited on the brick porch for the doorbell to be answered, the distinct odor of stale flowers and unwashed blankets drifted from a rocking chair at his side.

"Yes?" a weak voice asked from behind the door.

"Annabelle Bowman?"

"What do you want?"

"My name's Max Porter. I was hoping I could talk to you for a few minutes. I have a few questions for an article I'm researching."

The door opened a crack. "Article?"

Max flashed his warmest smile as he peeked in at the elderly woman. "Yes, I'm writing an article for, um, I don't know yet. It's kind of a freelance thing."

"Freelance?"

"It means that I don't have —"

"I know what it means, you idiot. Sure, what the hell, I ain't had anything interesting happen in months," she said, nudging the door open and shuffling toward her living room. "Besides, I don't think I've got to worry about you raping me, and there ain't anything here worth stealing."

Max stepped inside to find a home cramped with books, statuettes, and trinkets of all kinds. Next to a mirror, a framed cross-stitching hung on the wall declaring "Home is life." Two overstuffed sofas dominated the living room. A coffee table covered with photos of young children, sat between them.

"My nieces and nephews," she said.

"They look lovely."

"The one in the green shirt is. The other two are a pain but they'll outgrow it. And this picture is my sister, Emily. I haven't heard from her in awhile. Her husband thinks I'm a bit of a bitch, I suppose. Excuse my language. I used to be more refined but at my age, you start to realize all that politeness doesn't get you very far. Better to be honest and direct, even if it does piss off a few people along the way."

Max chuckled as he sat. "I won't take up too much of your time," he said.

"I'm not going anywhere. Would you like some sweet tea?"

"No, thank you," he said. Sweet tea was everywhere in North Carolina, but for Max's northern tastes it was much too sweet, not enough tea.

"What do you want to talk about?" Annabelle asked.

"Well, I saw a picture of you in a story about Millionaire's Row."

Annabelle snorted a laugh which fast turned into a rasping cough. "What in Heaven do you care about all that?"

"I just found it interesting. It's not everyday that a bunch of people wake up instant millionaires — sort of like winning the lottery."

"Loyalty gets rewarded sometimes," she said, pulling a knitted blanket over her lap. "Even if the reward comes from a bastard."

"Would that be F. Ross Johnson?"

"Those families had all worked for Reynolds Tobacco for most of their lives. They were loyal to the company. They bought stock in it. Reynolds made this town, y'know? Then suddenly the company becomes RJR Nabisco, and that wasn't so bad at first, but Johnson screwed us all — sent the headquarters off to Atlanta. I swear, if lynching had been legal, I don't think Johnson would've lasted the week."

Max nodded. "And then he let the whole thing be taken over in a leveraged buyout."

"That's right. Forced us to sell our shares. We all made a lot of money, sure, but it never was about money. You listen to me. Money's always been an illusion," she said, her eyes glancing at her hands with a mournful hesitancy. She cracked a smile and said, "You know, when the reporters all showed up, they thought they'd get pictures of us hicks spending lavishly on new cars and new houses and diamond rings and such. Instead, they got us. We all still live in the same homes — those of us still alive, that is — and we all go on the same way. We just plunked the money into savings and that was that. So, there's not much of a story here for you."

"Actually," Max said as a nervous throbbing built in his chest, "I did have one little item I hoped you could clear up for me."

"Oh?" she said, her smile turning into a sharp, controlled line.

"It's about your stock. See, according to the newspapers, all the others had bought their stock in small bits over the years of their employment. You, however, never worked for Reynolds. I was just wondering why you would have followed the same pattern as they did."

"My late husband worked for them."

"That would be Stan Bowman?"

"I think you should leave now," Annabelle said, heading for the front door.

The chill that blew into the room struck Max hard. He never had been in this type of situation, and he found himself wishing Drummond could have come along. The aid of a real detective appeared quite attractive at the moment.

"Please, I didn't mean to upset you. I'm just trying to find out —"

"I know what you want. Now, I'm very busy today, so please leave or I'll have to call the police."

"Do you know the name Hull?"

Annabelle stopped. She turned her eyes onto Max with such authority that he half-expected her to demand his hand for a ruler beating. "Whatever you're doing looking into all of this, you better stop it. This city was built on the backs of old families like Hull, Hanes, and Reynolds. You've got to understand that. R. J. Reynolds Tobacco — it's not just a company or a stock, it's a religion. And you don't go messing with somebody's religion."

Chapter 7

DRUMMOND BOUNCED AROUND THE OFFICE, clapped his hands together, and nodded. "Damn, I wish I could've been there," he said, rubbing his mouth. "And I wish I could have a cigarette."

"Sorry, I don't smoke," Max said, slumping in his chair. Sweat still dampened his armpits and his fingers still trembled from all the adrenaline pumping through him. He could hear the menace behind the old lady's voice echoing in his head.

"I'm dead, remember? I don't have lungs to smoke with. She really said all that, huh? It's a religion?"

"Yeah, she said that."

"And you just left?"

"She obviously wanted me to go."

"Of course she did. She knows something. She wanted you out as fast as possible. And that's important because it means somewhere inside her, she knows that she can be pushed into blabbing her secrets."

"It does?"

"Always. Somebody with nothing to hide or somebody who knows he'll never crack, people like that will let you hang out and talk for hours. They don't care. They want to spin you in circles. But the ones that throw you out, those are the gold mines."

Max glanced at the book with the hidden flask but shook his head. "Look, this is all getting nutty. I mean, I took the job with Hull because I needed the money. I'm supposed to be looking up land deals and old history. Now I don't know what you've brought me into."

Drummond halted and stared hard into Max. "You don't get to back out of things like this. You better start understanding that. It doesn't matter what your intentions were or how you ended up here, the fact is that you *are* here. You do know things now that companies like Hull are not going to be happy about. So shut up and start thinking."

"About what?"

"Our next step, of course. You really have no clue what you're doing, do you?"

"Fine," Max said, crossing his arms and spinning his chair so he could pout toward the window. "Tell me, then, what is our next great step?"

"Well, we could follow Annabelle. You could, I mean. Whenever you shake up somebody like this, really throw them for a loop, they usually start acting on whatever it is they're hiding. You follow her and you might learn something."

"No."

"What?"

"I'm not a detective. I do research and I teach. I don't go following people around, taking their pictures, and seeing what they're up to."

Drummond passed through the desk and settled in front of Max. "You must be a great lover or hung like an elephant or something because I can't see what your wife sees in you."

"Thanks," Max said, plastering a sarcastic grin on his face. "You really know how to speak to my heart."

Drummond stared at Max for awhile without saying a word. Max stared back, wondering if this had become a game of chicken or if Drummond actually had started thinking about the case again. With another clap of his hands, Drummond broke the silence and said, "Okay. You say you're the research man, then let's do some research."

"What now?"

"Stocks. You said Annabelle made a fortune in Reynolds stock, right?"

"That's right."

"But she never worked for the company, and after what had occurred with her husband, you'd think she would never want anything from them. Not to mention that unless she had some rich uncle or something, she and Stan did not have much in the way of money."

Max spun back to his desk. "So where did the stock come from?"

"Exactly."

"She could've bought it in small amounts over the years like the others. Maybe figured RJR owed her something."

"True, but she threw you out of her house."

With a drum roll on the table, Max said, "I'll see what I can find out."

"Good," Drummond said. "But before you do all that, you ought to be ready for Modesto."

"What about him?"

"I just saw him walk into the building."

"Great," Max said, took a deep breath, and opened a notebook. "You stay quiet," he said and attempted to look busy. Drummond exaggerated locking his mouth as he floated toward the ceiling. Max chilled at the display but said nothing. He had to start getting comfortable with ghostly ways.

A moment later, Modesto opened the door and took a

seat without a word. Max lifted a halting finger, pretended to take a few final notes, and then raised his head with a smile. "Mr. Modesto, it's always good to see you." Modesto glared at Max but showed no sign of talking. "Something you want? I didn't think I had to give a report for a few more days. I suppose if you need something now —"

"I'm not here for a report."

Drummond drifted against the bookshelf and squinted as he scrutinized Modesto. "Be careful, Max. He knows something."

"I can see that," Max said, trying to keep his eyes on Modesto, though he kept catching Drummond in his peripheral vision. "Perhaps you could save us some time and tell me why you're here?"

"Why were you talking to Annabelle Bowman?" Modesto asked, crossing his legs with calm power.

"Don't tell him anything," Drummond said.

"I know how to do my job," Max said.

Modesto gestured toward the desk corner. "You don't appear to understand how to follow instructions."

Using every ounce of self-control he could muster, Max refused to look at the desk corner. "What do you mean?" he asked, knowing that he sounded guiltier than ever.

"You were asked to research the early foundations of this town in order to help us acquire important historical pieces of land. Annabelle Bowman has nothing to do with that."

Drummond stepped in between the men and faced Modesto. He squatted down and said, "You better come up with something quick, Max, and it better be good. I don't think he'll buy much malarkey."

Max reached into his pocket and pushed the vibrate button on his cell phone. Acting startled, he pulled the phone out, checked the face, and said, "Excuse me, one moment."

"Of course," Modesto said.

Max flipped open the phone and said, "Hi, how are you?"

Drummond looked back at Max. "Is there really a call?"

"No, no."

"I see, buying time, huh?"

"Not quite."

"Then what?"

"Look, I'm in an important meeting right now, and I'm not trying to be rude or anything but you're interrupting," Max said. He covered the phone and said to Modesto, "Just a minute longer. Sorry about this."

"I can wait," Modesto said.

Drummond pulled up and stomped off to the corner, stepping through Modesto in the process. Modesto shivered. "I'm just trying to help," Drummond said.

"I know," Max said. "I do. It's just a bit difficult to carry on more than one conversation at a time. I'll call you after my meeting, okay?"

"Not okay. You need me. You screwed up with Annabelle, and you'll screw up here."

"I've really got to go."

"Fine," Drummond said and turned around showing only his back to Max.

Max put the cell phone away and said to Modesto, "Sorry about that. Now, you were asking about Annabelle Bowman. I suppose I understand your confusion in the matter. You're not an expert at research. And, well, I admit I acted a bit too enthusiastically. You had mentioned land deals being our ultimate objective, so I jumped ahead. See, history books will only help us out so much. If I'm to find quality pieces of real estate for our employer then I need to talk to the people who might own such pieces."

"And you think Ms. Bowman is such a person?"

"Well, she did become very wealthy, very quickly. Usually people who win the lottery or inherit a ton of money will buy up some local properties as a place to plunk down all this wealth they don't know what to do with. That's why I spoke to her."

"Why didn't you talk to any of the other stockholders who made it big off of Reynolds?"

"I intend to. Ms. Bowman was merely my first stop. I'm afraid it didn't go too well, she's very cranky, so I decided to rethink my approach before I tackled another."

Drummond spun around. "I can't take this. Ask him the crucial question, already!"

Max continued, "I do have a question for you, though."

"Oh? And what is that?"

Nobody said anything for a moment. Modesto looked at Max expectantly, and then said, "Mr. Porter? Do you have a question or not?"

"Gee," Drummond said, striding back to the desk. "I guess you might need my help after all, huh?"

"Yes," Max said.

Modesto opened his arms. "I can't wait all day."

Drummond shook his head. "Ask him how he knew you saw Annabelle Bowman today."

Sitting straighter, his heart jumping as the question sunk in, Max said, "I'm curious about something. How is that you know I saw Ms. Bowman today? I never told anybody I was going there. I never even indicated in my reports that I would be taking this approach. How is it that you know where I've been? Are you having me followed?"

For the first time, Max saw Mr. Modesto's cool exterior falter. It did not last long, but it scared Max. With a patience that added to Max's growing dread, Modesto stood and leaned on the table. "Yes, I've had you followed. The library trips, lunches with your wife, visits to old rich ladies. I've had people watching you since before you moved here. And I will continue to have you followed until I am convinced that you do not pose a threat to our employer's interests. That is what I am an expert at."

Max struggled to make his throat open enough for speaking. At length, he said, "I-I'm not trying to pick a fight with you. I just didn't like the idea. Listen, you have nothing to worry over with me."

Drummond walked right through the desk, waving his hands, and said, "Shut up. Don't say another word."

"I came down here because our employer offered me a lot of money," Max said. Now that he got himself talking, he found it harder to stop. "I don't have any interest in what he wants with the information I find. I just want my money and that'll be it. I don't care about him or anything like that. I won't go to the police, not that there's anything to go to the police with anyway."

Drummond covered his eyes. "Oh, please, shut up. Please."

The calculating expression on Modesto's face finally got Max quiet. Max tried to speak again but his lips only quivered. Modesto pulled back, donned his coat, and said, "Do your job, Mr. Porter." He slapped a manila envelope on the desk. "Research these properties, take your money, and move away from here. Anything else would be inadvisable."

"Yes, sir," Max managed as Modesto strolled away.

Once the stairwell door clanged shut, Drummond faced Max and said, "What the hell is the matter with you? I told you to ask him one simple question, not divulge every little nuance of your thought process, and certainly not to piss all over the man, and most definitely, most certainly, I did not tell you to mention the police."

"I didn't. I said I wouldn't involve the police."

"You mentioned them. That's enough. It shows that you think there's something illegal, something worth telling the police about."

"I didn't know."

"How could you not know? I've been a ghost for decades now, and even I've heard enough about modern cinema to know that every bum in this country should be aware of basic procedures in this kind of thing."

Max's shaking hands tightened into fists as his anger grew. "Well, things are a heck of a lot different when you're actually in the situation."

"You've got that much right," Drummond said as he sat down and lifted his legs onto the desk. "You know, I think I'd love a cigarette more right now than life itself."

Maybe it was the sudden shift in attitudes or maybe Max had begun to like the gruff detective, he didn't know. Either way, Max could not resist pointing to Drummond's feet. "How do you do that? Put your feet on the desk or clap your hands or anything like that?"

Drummond shrugged. "I just do. When I want to go through something, I do it. When I want to be more substantial, I can do that too."

"So, now I guess we look into that stock information?"

"It's not too late to stakeout Ms. Annabelle."

Max's cell phone buzzed — Sandra. "Hi, honey," Max said while scowling at Drummond. "I'm fine ... well, today's been interesting ... I've still got some research to do ... sure, honey, if it's important, I'll be there ... oh, I see."

"Well?" Drummond said to Max's stunned face.

"My wife has informed me that we have a date tonight."

"A date? With your wife? You're married to her but you're still dating? Oh, hell, the 1940s made a lot more sense."

Chapter 8

MAX DISLIKED LOW-PRICED RESTAURANTS because all the families with obnoxious kids ate at such places. With their finances strapped, however, he and Sandra had little choice in the matter if they wanted to eat out. So, as Max bit into the dry turkey and over-ripe tomato of his club sandwich, he listened to a four-year-old scream "Mine! Mine! Mine!" while the sweet darling's adoring parents smacked him across the head.

Sandra cracked a grin and shrugged. "It could be worse."

"Really?" Max said, thinking about the day he had endured and how little of it he dared to share with his wife.

"Sure. That kid could be ours."

This elicited a slight chuckle. A moment later, they settled into silence and ate. Max wanted to relax, to pay attention, to be a good date, but he could not stop thinking about Drummond, Bowman, Modesto, and Hull. Even if he had the courage to divulge a tiny portion of what had happened, Sandra could not possibly believe him — a detective ghost and office witchcraft and a forgotten madman.

"Come on," Sandra said, her voice soft yet firm. "Please try to have a good time."

"What? Oh, no, I'm fine. Just a bit preoccupied."

"Honey, I know you don't like your job, but you've got

to deal with it."

"I am," Max said, snapping harder than he had intended. He drank some soda through a straw and continued, "I've just had a stressful day, that's all."

"Okay, okay. I'm sorry."

The brat screaming "Mine! Mine! Mine!" hit the high-point of his meltdown. He sprawled on the floor and wailed. Two haggard parents scooped him up, dodging his flailing arms, and lugged him outside. Sandra could not hold back her laughter.

"It's not funny," Max said. "Those are horrible parents and they have no consideration for anybody else."

Sandra whooped a short laugh and regained her composure. "You could really use a hard drink, couldn't you?"

Max sipped his straw again, making a silly face that sent Sandra into more hysterics. "So let me ask you something," Max said, deciding at that very moment upon a way to lightly dance atop the explosives that had become his life. "Do you believe in ghosts?"

Wiping her eyes, Sandra said, "Ghosts?"

"Spirits of the dead. Y'know, ghosts."

Sandra took a long drink, giving Max the impression that she was stalling. "Yes, I suppose I do. Why are you even asking?"

Waving away the question, Max said, "Forget it. How was your day?"

"Fine," Sandra said with a touch of relief. "Actually, I'm still having problems with my boss, but it's nothing to worry about."

"We both have boss problems, then."

"And we'll both persevere. Now, let's talk no more of work and bosses and anything like that."

"Okay. What do you want to talk about?"

Sandra opened her mouth but said nothing. Then, with a shake of her head, she started to laugh again. They enjoyed the rest of their meal, talking about a television show, Max's mother, and something Sandra heard on the radio. Savoring the weightlessness of the evening, they both relaxed for an hour.

Max would later recall two sounds as they headed toward their car in the brisk night air. First, he heard the crunching of heavy feet in the gravel — a sound that spoke of urgency and threat. The second sound, however, would be forever chiseled into his being — Sandra's terror-filled scream as two men wearing ski-masks shoved her aside and assaulted Max.

They each took one of his arms and threw him against the restaurant's wall. The cold brick scratched into his back as one of the men, the heavier one, punched Max in the gut. The other one pulled out a handgun that shined its metallic blue under the parking lot lights and pointed it at Sandra. Max gasped for enough air to speak, his lungs burning and his stomach stuck in a tight clench, but he only managed to cough up phlegm.

The heavy man grabbed Max's hair and wrenched his head back. Max could see Sandra shaking, her face looking upon him, terrified she might never see him again. He wanted to reach out to her, to give her some assurance they would be fine, but the gun pointed at her head kept him wondering.

"Stop looking into things that don't matter anymore," the heavy man said, his breath reeking of alcohol. Another punch to the gut and a kick in the side capped off the performance. Then the two men dashed off into the darkness. As Max rolled to his side, Sandra raced over and wrapped her arms around him.

She whispered words he could not decipher, and he

knew the words were more for her own comfort than his. After a few minutes, his stomach muscles loosened a little, and he found the strength to stand. Pain shot from his side. He prayed they hadn't broken his ribs — paying for medical care was not a line item in the Porter budget.

Later, in their kitchen, Sandra helped Max ease out of his shirt. He winced and groaned but managed.

"That looks pretty bad," she said, placing an icepack over the purple/black bruise on his side.

"Easy," he said, hissing air as he lowered his arm onto the icepack.

"Don't be a baby."

"I got kicked in the ribs!"

"And I had a gun to my head," Sandra said, slamming a second icepack onto the table. Her hands shook, and her face quivered as tears welled in her eyes. She rubbed them away and returned to checking his wounds.

"We're okay now. We can relax. It's all over."

"No, it's not. You know that. I heard what he said to you. This was just a warning."

"They may not even have had the right guy."

"Bullshit! They targeted you and you know it," Sandra said and the two locked eyes like poker players attempting to cover all sense of meaning in their expressions. Breaking away, Sandra fixed a glass of cola for Max and said, "Doesn't look like you've got any broken bones."

"At least that much is good."

"Sure," she said, the sarcasm dripping heavy and thick, "real good. Just wonderful, in fact. We ought to get attacked more often."

Max sipped his cola and said, "I know it was scary and all, but it's over."

"Stop saying that. I'm not a child and I'm not a fool. This was a warning. To you. This is all because of

Drummond, isn't it? It is. I can see it in your face. So, you tell me right now, what's going on?"

Despite her stern mouth, Max saw the fear dancing on her skin. He knew exactly how she felt. He felt it, too. Anger strong enough to tear down walls. Fear powerful enough to keep him frozen.

"I don't know if it's the Drummond thing. I don't. Honest. I mean it probably is, but I don't know one hundred percent for sure. But come on, now, this shouldn't be such a shock."

"What?"

"We both know something's not right about my employer."

"What are you saying?"

Max gestured to the chair opposite him and waited for her to sit. Sandra glanced at the chair; then leaned against the counter. "It's truth time," he said. "Okay? Don't you think? No more pretending. We've both kept quiet about it. We've both ignored all the red flags smacking us in the face because we wanted the money, the security. We wanted to get out of the mess in Michigan."

"You made that mess."

"I'm not trying to dredge up all that. I just —"

Sandra shook her head as she pulled a beer from the refrigerator. "I see how you want this," she said. "It's truth time but only when you've got something to say."

"No, I just didn't want us to rehash an old fight."

"Well, we're here, right now, talking about all of this because of that old fight. Maybe we should consider finishing it this time."

Never before had Max seen his wife carry such a harsh expression. Disgust and hatred filled him at the sight — not for her but towards himself. He had caused her to look that way. If this was "truth time," then he had to start with himself. "Okay," he said. "Michigan was my fault, and I think all of this is my fault, too."

Sandra drank her beer as she settled into her chair. Then, with a tired yet still boiling tone, she said, "They accused you of sleeping with a student, and I believe whole-heartedly you didn't do it. So, let's start with that. I want to know why you let them fire you. And don't tell me how you hated your boss and the legal costs were too high and all those other excuses you've used before. I want to know the truth. Why didn't you fight for that job?"

Max closed his eyes and nodded. "It's funny, I always tell myself it happened because of the boss thing or that my ideas were stolen or a number of other excuses. Truth is, though, I deserved to be fired. That's why I didn't fight. I knew if we fought back, they'd look into my work, my files, everything. They'd poke into everything, and eventually they'd learn that I *had* done something wrong. Not what they accused me of, I never slept with a student, but something that could've landed me in jail."

"What did you do?" Sandra asked, her voice quiet and frightened like a girl being told her mommy was being arrested.

Max swallowed hard. "I found a loophole in their computer accounting system. I was talking with the principal one day and it was just there on her desk and she was nowhere and I don't know what I was thinking, but I just reached over and made a few checks for CASH."

"You embezzled from a school?"

"We were freezing to death, for crying out loud. I'm sorry I'm not the great provider, but I had to do something. And really, isn't that why we're here? We hated how hard our lives were back there. We hated it. All the time, we complained and griped and it was ripping us to pieces. We barely talked about anything else. Then, this job landed in my lap and we saw the dollar signs and that was it, no questions."

"It wasn't like that."

"No, no. This is truth time. We *both* accepted that there was something odd about this job. We both knew it was not on the up-and-up."

Indignation flashed in Sandra's eyes, only to be replaced by calm acceptance. A single tear escaped her tight control, and with a trembling voice, she asked, "How bad is it this time? Are you going to go to jail?"

"What? No. I've done nothing wrong. I'm just researching old history looking for buildings. That's it. But obviously, there's more to all this than real estate deals."

"Obviously."

Max shifted in his chair and fire swelled from his bruises and seared up his side. "It's all crazy. I've actually been thinking how nice Michigan was."

"Michigan was a crappy mess."

"My point exactly." Max dropped his hands to his lap. "I've just got to get through the job. Just do the research, get my check, and then I'll quit. I'll walk away."

"Honey, you're not thinking. When does somebody ever get to walk away from people like this?"

"But I don't know anything."

"Does that really matter? What you need to do is quit all this Drummond business, do your job, and keep your mouth shut and your ears open. We need to find some way to get out, something to hold over their heads."

"Are you crazy? These people sent two men to beat me up. They had a gun to your head."

"I haven't forgotten," Sandra said, her anger erupting as tears streamed out unchecked. "But we can't just sit back and wait for you to piss them off enough to kill us. You need to do something. You don't like my idea, fine. You tell me, then. What can we do?"

Max sagged in his chair. He knew all along this question was coming, and he knew the answer. "You won't like it," he said and finished his drink, the clinking ice cubes underscoring his soft words.

"I don't like any of this."

"I'm going to help Drummond. I know that seems nuts to you, but there's more to it than you know, and if I can find out what happened to ... what happened, then maybe I'll have that missing something you want me to find. Something to protect us from my employer."

"But all of this started with Drummond. Why help him?"

"I think his case is connected to everything else. At least, I'm pretty sure it is."

"Okay, okay. But, honey, I'm scared."

"Me, too," Max said.

Sandra took a shaking breath and placed her hand on the table. Max reached out, and they held hands in the kitchen without another word.

Chapter 9

THE NEXT MORNING, after overcoming the difficulty of taking a shower and driving to work with half his body throbbing in pain, Max opened his office door to discover a tall, blonde man moving papers on his desk. He was young, perhaps still in college, and had a boyish smooth face. He looked up, adjusted his glasses, stood, and offered his hand.

"Are you Mr. Porter?" the young man asked with a slight drawl. He pushed his thin hair back, but in moments it had swooped down to cover his right eye once again.

Max shook the hand. "I am. And this is my office, though that doesn't seem to matter to anybody around here."

"I'm sorry. I was told to let myself in. My name's Taylor. Mr. Modesto hired me to be your assistant."

Drummond slipped out of the bookcase and started shouting. "Can you believe this? A damn spy. I tried to get this idiot to leave. I've been knocking books to the floor and throwing papers around, but the prick won't go."

Taylor moved around the desk, his hands jittering as he pointed at Drummond. "I think that bookshelf is not flush with the floor. Things keep slipping out of it."

Drummond stomped around the room. "I'm sick of him. He's been here less than an hour and I can't stand him. If only I could deck him. I know, I know, but that's it for me — books are the biggest thing I've been able to move. Kind of stings, too, but for this clown, I'll suffer it."

Max tried to ignore Drummond for the moment. "You said that Mr. Modesto hired you?"

"Yes, sir," Taylor said. "I'm to help you however you need. He said you were doing research."

"Um, there's been a misunderstanding. I don't require an assistant."

Drummond slapped another book to the floor. As Taylor placed it back, he said, "Mr. Modesto said you'd say that. He told me that I had to stay even if you tried to fire me. He said only he could fire me. I'm sorry, sir, but I need this job. It pays really well and college is expensive. And, frankly, there isn't much else out there. So, if you don't put me to work, I'm supposed to just sit here." With that, Taylor took the left guest chair, looking more uncomfortable than before.

"I see," Max said. "I guess I'll work elsewhere today."

"Excuse me, sir?"

"What?" Drummond asked.

Max stepped to the side so that he could face both Taylor and Drummond while speaking to Taylor. "I don't mean to offend you. Mr. Modesto can hire you to do whatever he wants. He cannot, however, force me to accept it. I'll do my work elsewhere. Please leave by five and be sure to lock the door."

Drummond walked right through Taylor in his desperate approach to Max. "Don't do this. It's bad enough being stuck in this room all day, but don't leave him here with me."

Taylor appeared to be working a complex problem in his head when Max opened the office door. "Goodbye," he said and walked out.

The lady living down the hall stepped out for her

newspaper. She eyed Max as he said, "Good morning."

As Max reached the end of the hall, Taylor exclaimed, "This is a test, ain't it? Don't worry, sir, I'll be right here to five o'clock. You can count on me."

The lady cocked an eyebrow. Embarrassed, Max said, "New assistant. He's a bit overenthusiastic." With a grunt, the lady closed her door.

Max had two distinct impressions of Taylor. One — he was like any other college kid and would goof around all day unless Max stayed in the office. And two — Drummond was right. Whether the kid knew it or not, he had been hired to spy. That last idea sent nervous tingling through Max's skin, but not because he feared its veracity — rather, Max chilled at how easily he accepted the idea of being spied upon. *I'm starting to know my enemy.*

By the time he reached Wake (and after seven minutes of searching for a parking space), he had formulated his next few steps. First, when he entered the library, he found a private corner and sent an e-mail to Roddy, his pal in Michigan. They had been college roommates, and Max hoped he could still trust the man. Before moving to Michigan, Roddy had worked on Wall Street, and Max's e-mail asked Roddy to draw on those old days to get any information about Annabelle Bowman's stock acquisitions. With the e-mail sent off, Max started his own research on local land deals.

The work kept Max's mind from wandering which kept him from worrying. Hours passed by in research bliss until he had to admit that all his work had turned up no results. According to all the records he could find, nobody named Hull ever owned any land in Winston-Salem. While certainly odd, it was not unfathomable. The Hull's could have numerous dummy corporations set up to hold the land. Such things were done all the time in order to protect family money from litigation damages.

With a loud gurgle, Max's stomach protested the long day. His watch read 3:30, so he hurried over to Benson University Center to grab a quick bite among the students. No sooner had he left the library than his cell phone chirped — his mother.

"Hi, Mom," Max said as he weaved around students.

"Hi, dear."

"I can't talk long. I've got to get some lunch before I get back to work."

"Oh, that's nice. Your work is going well?"

Max sighed. "Yes. It's fine."

"And how's Sandra?"

"She's doing well. Loves it down here."

"I'm so glad. As long as you two are happy than the rest of it doesn't matter."

Here it was. Max tried to refrain from taking the bait but he had to ask, "The rest of what?"

"Oh, never mind. I'm just an old woman all by myself waiting for her grandchildren."

Bingo! Grandchildren. "I know. But we can barely afford to keep ourselves going. A child is way too expensive."

"Your father and I did fine with you, didn't we?"

"Yes, Mom."

"Times were harder then. So, enough excuses. You talk with that wife of yours and get some children. Why on Earth get married if you didn't want kids? It's beyond me."

"Okay, I'll do that," Max said as he stepped into Benson University Center. "I have to go now. I have to eat."

"Are you eating well?"

"I'm trying."

"It's important. Lucas Hoffmeyer died last week because he stopped eating well. Of course, he was ninety-two but still, you have to take care of your body. Do you know I used to bring Lucas meals and read to him and things like that?"

Max dumped his things at the nearest available table, resigned to the fact that he would not get to eat until the phone conversation ended, and that would only happen when his mother decided it would happen. "No, Mom, I don't think I knew that."

"Well, I did," she said, her pride boosting every word. "He would call me 'one of his gals' and he'd tell me stories of his youth. Remarkably warm, gracious man. I really enjoyed talking with him. Oh, and his grandfather, you wouldn't believe the stories about his grandfather. Why the man served during the Civil War! Can you imagine that?"

But Max had stopped listening. The Civil War. Something about it clicked, and he found no internal resistance to interrupting his mother. "Mom, I have to go. I'll try to call you later. Bye," he said and closed the cell phone before she could say another word. Without bothering for food, Max rushed back to the library, his excitement held in check only by the odd looks he received from passing students.

The Civil War. The Hull family may have covered their tracks with dummy corporations now but back during the Civil War? He doubted they would have been so thorough back then. They would have tried but deleting files is different from hunting down every scrap of paper with the name Hull written upon it.

In less than an hour, Max had sifted through the entire roster of Civil War participants from the Winston-Salem area. It had been a fascinating experience in itself, but more so because of what he discovered. The name Hull came up several times often accompanied by the phrase "of the prominent family" or "married into the notable family" or even in one case, "proud grandchild of the great family." In each instance, Max wrote down the name and any particulars provided. He then began researching land deals from the Civil War era. As dinnertime neared, his unappeased hunger rebelled against his enthusiastic curiosity, and he had to admit that he had come up empty. All those "prominent" Hulls, yet not a single one owned any property.

After shoving down a burger and offering an apologetic call to Sandra, Max shuffled into his office. His watch beeped the arrival of seven o'clock, and thankfully, his new assistant had followed orders. Max dropped into his chair and said, "So, how was your day?"

Drummond stepped out of the far wall, his shoulders raised and his face scrunched. Through clenched teeth, he said, "You must get rid of that bastard."

Max's body still ached, though not as bad as that morning. But the thought of dealing with a belligerent ghost caused many of his bruises to flare up. "I can't fire him and he won't budge."

"Do you know what he did all day while you were out? He opened that window and he smoked. He smoked! Oh, if that smell isn't the most intoxicating, I swear there's a Devil and it wants to torture me every chance it gets."

"I really am sorry. But I have no way."

"Yes, you do," Drummond said, sliding closer with a boyish twinkle. "I've been waiting for you to broach the subject, to even suggest it, but you've clearly got a lot of other things to worry about. Either that or you're a thoughtless bastard."

"I'm really tired. Whatever you want, can it —"

"I don't have to be stuck here."

"You don't?"

"Not at all," Drummond said, his eagerness beaming.

Max had so many little puzzle pieces refusing to fit together that playing a guessing game with Drummond held no appeal. "Just tell me," he said.

"I'm here because of a curse. You can change that. You can undo the curse and set me free. Then I can help you with the case, be right by your side the whole time."

"Oh, sure. That'd be great," Max said, picturing how impossible his research days would be with Drummond floating around the library making boisterous comments — *I'm bored — I want to smoke — Look at these co-eds.*

"Okay, okay, so I won't be by your side all day. The point is I can do more out there than I can stuck in here. Besides, if Hull wants me stuck here, shouldn't that say to you that I present more of a threat to them if I'm unstuck?"

Max yawned and said, "Hey, I've got no problem with the idea of setting you free. I do, however, have the problem of not having a clue how to do it, and while I know there's a book on that shelf about witchcraft, I find it highly unlikely that they would give me the curse-breaking spell so easily."

"You're right. That book won't help. In fact, you can't go to a book on witchcraft to help me. You have to go to a witch."

Max started shaking his head before Drummond finished speaking. "No, no, no. A witch? No. I am not going to ... no. I'm sorry but that is just ... no."

"Oh, come on," Drummond snapped. "I'm not asking you to give her your blood or something. Just find out what we need to do. That's it. Besides, she's a beautiful woman."

"What? Are you saying you know a witch? A real witch?"

Drummond gave a sly wink. "I knew her grandmother. Look, I promise it won't be any trouble. Just go to her house, explain who I am, tell her I need her help, and she'll help you out."

"She isn't the offspring of your illegitimate love-child or something?"

"Very funny. Now, come on, help me out."

"I wasn't joking."

Drummond stared at Max's pale face and pointed at him. "You're scared."

"I'm not scared."

"You are."

"I don't care about the witch. You want me to talk to her? Fine, I'll go talk to her. Okay?"

"No, you're scared. Maybe not of the witch, but of something. Me, maybe? You're worried that if you let me loose, I'll start haunting you."

"You already haunt me," Max said, trying to let the sarcasm ease his wounded nerves. "Really, though, I'm not scared. I've just got other things on my mind, that's all."

Drummond clapped his hands. "I see, now. You're scared that I'll just leave. Break the curse and your good pal, Marshall Drummond, the detective, will vanish forever."

"You highly overestimate yourself."

"I think you underestimate how dead-on I can be. Go see the witch, Max. And stop fretting. I'm not going away. Even if I didn't want revenge, I'd stick around. This is just too much fun."

Max tried to look away from Drummond, but the ghost kept floating before him. Drummond's eyes pleaded and smiled and harbored hope. Worse, Drummond was right. Max feared being alone in all of this. *But what right do I have to keep this man imprisoned?*

"Okay," he said.

Drummond put his arms out wide. "If I could, I'd hug you right now. Thank you. I promise I'll stick around. You've got my word as a detective and a ghost."

"Just tell me her name."

"Ashley Connor. You go see her tonight."

"Tonight?"

"Come now, my new partner, you're not going to make me stay stuck like this another whole day, are you?"

Like an old cop faced with yet another petty crime, Max donned his coat and said, "Fine, fine. Just give me the address."

Chapter 10

SITTING IN HIS CAR, staring at the two-story office building amongst many clones in the office park, Max shuddered. Across the street, somber brown signs with white lettering pointed to the dwellings of lawyers and dentists. An auto insurance salesmen used the bottom floor of the tan building Max had parked in front of, and just a few blocks over was Hanes Mall and the endless rows of chain stores built up around the shopping Mecca. In this little, tan building, if Drummond had told the truth, Max would find a witch — not somebody playing at being one with nature or hoping to pull off a few sparkly magic tricks, but an authentic witch. He shuddered again.

His mind kept dragging him back in time to the life of an eleven-year-old stuck in an apartment while the Michigan snows piled ever higher on the ground. School had been closed for two days and though Max's father risked his life to escape to work, his mother had been just as stuck as Max. At first, she attempted to entertain him, but he acted so moody that she left him alone most of the time. They would, however, sit together in front of the television for lunch — sipping soup and munching on grilled-cheese sandwiches. Max loved that tiny half-hour — the only minutes of the day his mother did not flit around the house cleaning, organizing, rearranging like a nervous animal convinced a predator lay in wait should anything be out of place.

The strangeness of the memory crept under his skin, jangling his nerves to a higher degree than his fear already had achieved. For now, that predator was a witch. A witch? How can this really be a witch? He never believed in such things. *Until last week, I never believed in ghosts, either.*

From his wallet, Max produced a picture of Sandra. He gave it a kiss and said, "I wish I could tell you all this, but even if you believed me, and I know you'd believe me, I don't want you getting caught up in it." He could hear her arguing back, saying that they were supposed to be a team, that the whole purpose of marriage was to form that team, and that he could never protect her from bad things by keeping her ignorant of them. "I know," he said to the picture as he placed it back in his wallet.

Max clapped his hands in a way that reminded him too much of Drummond, and he got out of the car. Everything looked cold — the empty parking spaces, the quiet night air, the pale parking lot lights. Even the simple, brown door carried a weight of threat.

Inside, he found a waiting room — one sofa, two chairs, boring coffee table with assorted magazines, jazz playing quietly from ceiling speakers, a few live plants dotting the corners, and framed photographs of deer and elk hung on the walls. A woman behind a counter like that in a doctor's office smiled at him and said, "Evening. How are ya?"

"I'm sorry. I think I'm at the wrong place."

"This is Dr. Ashley Connor's office," the woman said.

"Doctor?"

The woman kept her smile strong, but Max saw doubt entering her eyes. "Yes," she said, "Dr. Connor is an ophthalmologist."

"Oh, then I'm at the right place, I guess. Sorry for the

confusion. I've got a lot of doctor appointments this week. Trying to catch up on the backlog," he said, hoping to sound convincing.

"Are you Mr. Porter?"

"Yes?"

"She's got you down for a nine o'clock appointment."

"She does?"

"Yes, dear. Nine o'clock."

"Isn't it a bit late?"

"Certain appointments are considered of the highest priority."

"I see," he said, knowing he would regret asking the next question. "Except I didn't make an appointment. I was wondering how —"

"Everybody does. Now, if you'll just fill out this paperwork, we'll get you back there as soon as possible. Thank you."

Max took the clipboard the woman offered and sat on the leather sofa feeling like he just stepped out of a boxing ring after being pummeled in the head for ten rounds. How could she have written in an appointment when he hadn't even decided to go ahead with this until he left the car? How did she even know his name? Confusion painted every motion he made, but he pushed on despite his desire to run. He hated to admit it, but the more he thought over the possibilities, the more he agreed with Drummond — he needed the detective's help.

Fifteen minutes later, the receptionist sent him back to Room #4 where he found the traditional mechanical chair — several metal arms poked out of the side, each ending in a different tool. A hefty, attractive woman swept into the room and said with a thick Southern accent, "Good evening, Mr. Porter. I'm Julie."

"Good evening."

"You're new here. Where you from?"

"Michigan."

"Oh, that's much too cold for me," she said, as she turned down the lights and covered one of his eyes. With pleasant, pointless conversation, Julie tested Max's vision and finished by putting dilating drops into his eyes. "Dr. Connor will be in here in just a few minutes once those drops have a chance to work."

"Do you always stay open this late?"

"Only when we have special appointments, but then that happens a lot. Dr. Connor is very much in demand. It's a pleasure meeting you," Julie said and whisked out the door.

Max waited. Time crawled.

This is a stupid idea, he thought. Just taking the smallest step back and examining his recent circumstances, Max would have to admit that everything appeared crazy and dangerous. If he told anybody he was at the eye doctor waiting to talk to a witch about freeing a ghost so he could protect himself and his wife from an obsessive real estate developer — heck, just stating it in his head made him want to be committed.

As the impulse to leave gained enough momentum to raise Max from his chair, the door opened and in walked Dr. Ashley Connor. She was younger than Max, looked to be straight out of school, and her features reminded Max why college had been such a wonderful experience. Often when confronted with a beautiful woman, Max would half-jokingly say to himself, "Remember, you're married." This time, however, he found his mind altering the mantra to "Remember, she's a witch."

"Hello, Mr. Porter," Dr. Connor said as the light scent of rosemary perfume drifted toward Max. She closed the door and turned on the lights. Max winced — his dilated eyes unable to see her well in the brightness. The blurry image took him by the hand and headed toward the backend of the room. "Do I understand correctly that you wish to see me not as a doctor, but in a different capacity?"

"That's right," Max said, shading his eyes with one free hand. "I want to discuss an old friend of your grandmother."

"Just wait, please. We'll get to it all."

Dr. Connor opened a door Max had not noticed earlier and escorted him through a brightly lit passage to a round room covered in items. Max squinted, trying to see what the things hanging on the walls and stacked on the floor might be, but everything was a blurry confusion. Dr. Connor placed him by a stool, asked him to sit, and settled on another stool just far enough away that he only saw the fuzzy outline of her shape.

"This is about Marshall Drummond," she said.

"How did you know that?" Max asked. "And how did you know I was going to be here today?"

Dr. Connor leaned forward and whispered, "Because I'm the real thing, Mr. Porter."

"Then I guess I don't need to bother telling you the problem, and you can just give me whatever I need to help Drummond get free."

Though Max could not make out the doctor's face, he had no doubt she wore a broad smirk. She said, "You don't really think this would be that easy, do you? I'm a witch, after all. I don't just give things away. You have to pay for them."

"Something tells me we're not talking about money."

"Now you're starting to think. I make plenty of money as an eye doctor, and it keeps the IRS off my back. But the witch business — there never seems to be an end to people calling for these talents."

"So, what exactly —"

With a swift stroke, Dr. Connor cut the back of Max's hand. Before he had time to do more than jump a little, she scraped something across the wound and settled back as if nothing had happened. "That will do for a start," she said.

"What did you do to me?"

"Nothing bad. Not yet. Just a little insurance. After all, your kind have a long history of poorly treating my kind. So I now have a small sample of your blood. If you ever attempt to hurt me, there's a lot I can do to you with just a few drops."

"Don't you dare threaten me," Max said as sweat trembled out of his body. He tried to keep a brave outward appearance, tried to think of cool Drummond on a case facing some thugs, and it helped a bit.

Dr. Connor walked behind Max and stroked his hair. She then plucked out a few strands. "No threats. Just insurance."

"Fine. You've got your insurance. So, how do I get Drummond out of that office?"

"We're not there yet."

Max swallowed back his anger and unclenched his jaw. "I am not going to play games."

"It's all games. You can't even see five feet in front of you. You have no concept of who it is you're fighting against or what they're capable of. Because of your dear wife —"

"You stay away from her."

"— you're in a highly vulnerable position. You have high debt and the only money you're receiving is from a man you don't even know, let alone trust. It may just be my opinion, but I think you'd be best off to do whatever I say."

Though he hated hearing his weaknesses pointed out, he had to admit their validity. Even without the eye drops, he had been traipsing through his days blind and ignorant. He felt like the tail of a kite being whipped around in a heavy wind, unable to know what direction events would lead, just hanging on tight.

But it doesn't have to be this way. Drummond could help him get ahead for a change.

"Fine," he said. "What do we do next?"

"Next, you take off your clothes and make love to me."

"What?"

"Just kidding. Though I should tell you I don't care about marriage as an institution. If you ever feel like a little variety, I'd be interested."

Dr. Connor sat again, this time holding a book in her lap. "Let's see now," she said, and her tone told Max that this was going to go on for awhile longer. A loud buzz interrupted his thoughts and Dr. Connor scowled — at least, Max thought she scowled.

She walked to her wall and pushed a button. "What is it?"

"Mrs. Seaton is here."

"Thank you," she said, took a breath and sauntered back to her seat. "Okay, Mr. Porter, you might be having some luck tonight. Seems I'm a bit crunched for time. Everybody needs the help of a strong witch. Your friend, Drummond, has been put under a fairly simple binding curse. The markings used to keep him in one place have to be locked into a book or a scroll or something similar by copying the image on your floor into whatever item was chosen. To break the curse, you need to get ahold of the item, bring it to your office, and destroy it in the center of the floor marking. Understand?"

"I got it. Except how do we know where this copy is?"

"You just ask me."

"Okay, I'm asking. What do I need and where is it?"

"You go back to work now," Dr. Connor said with odd

precision. "Please inform Mr. Drummond that when he is ready to talk with me, then I will gladly share with him the information you require."

"Wait a second."

"Good-bye, now," she said and placed her hand on his head.

When Max opened his eyes, he was alone and in his car. His head throbbed. His muscles tightened as a rage built, but he clamped it down — no use getting angry just yet. He couldn't go back to the office, though. The idea of talking with Drummond ticked him off too much. He'd end up saying something he would no doubt regret. Instead, he drove home.

Chapter 11

"YOU HAD ME WORRIED," Sandra said as she refilled Max's coffee mug. "I can't even think of a time you've been out so late before. Maybe in college. And when you got home, you just crashed."

Max's head pounded as if he had drunk whiskey all night. The coffee perked him up a little, but his dry mouth and aching bones made him want to crawl back to bed.

"You better get out of those clothes," Sandra said.

"Sorry," he mumbled.

"It's okay. It's just that with everything that's happened, I was really worried. I'm just glad you're okay."

"I should've called," Max said as he slipped off his clothes and hunted for something clean to wear. "It all came down real quick. I'm sorry."

"I said it was okay."

"Thanks for the coffee."

"No problem." She stopped at the bedroom door. Before she spoke, Max's heart quickened — it knew what she would ask next, and it feared the question. "What exactly were you doing last night?"

He could hear the tenseness, the worry, the battle between the need to be comforted that all was well in their relationship and the terror that things might be as she suspected. A little assurance was all she sought. However, that required Max to tell her not to worry, that all was well — to lie. He couldn't tell her that he had been to see a witch. Would she even believe him? And offering anything simply to acknowledge that he wasn't having an affair would bring up further questions.

"Just work," he said, hearing his shallow lie.

"Oh," she said, that one utterance carrying far more disturbing depths.

"I have to go," he said, rushing downstairs, ignoring the pain in his body, and wishing he could do something to protect Sandra from her false belief.

By the time he reached his office, his horrible mood soured more. Taylor did his best to make matters worse. He offered an exuberant greeting and a cup of coffee. The coffee smelled delicious but Max had no intention of giving the boy any form of encouragement. He took the coffee, grunted, and plopped down at his desk. Before he could finish the first, sweet sip, Drummond appeared — cranky, as usual.

"Oh, the King finally decides to show up," Drummond said, kicking the furniture and acting as if he were destroying it instead have passing right through. "I cannot believe you care so little that you would keep me stuck here all night and tortured by this bastard kid all morning. I swear I've got it in me not to help you at all. Then where'd you be? Huh? You'd be a dead man. Your wife, too."

Max put the coffee cup down too hard and Taylor glanced up from paper sorting on the floor. "Everything okay, sir?"

"Fine," Max said.

"Not fine," Drummond went on. "Not fine, not one iota. Get me out of here, Max. Send this cretin packing and get me free."

Max crossed his arms and leaned back in his chair. With

a shocked gasp, Drummond said, "This a joke? You won't help me? For crying out loud, I'm sorry. Okay? I'm just anxious. Please, pull out your phone, so we can have a conversation."

The slim line of Max's mouth curled just a bit. Listening to Drummond whine had brightened his morning, and despite the pounding in his head, the aches in his muscles, or even the consistent pressure mounting on all sides, Max found the discomfort of a ghost amusing. However, the longer Drummond persisted, the more Max saw the play as cruel rather than simple teasing. "Taylor," he said. "I've got a terrible headache. Do me a favor, please, and get me some ibuprofen or something."

"Sure, sir," Taylor said and stepped into the bathroom. "I don't see nothing here. Where else would you have them?"

Snapping his fingers, Max said, "Oh, that's right, I must be all out. Will you please go downstairs and get me some? There's a convenience store on the street. I'm sure you'll find something in there."

Taylor hesitated. The tug-o-war between this request and the overriding rules set out by their mutual employer battled on his face. Max sensed that Taylor was going to refuse, so he added, "Taylor, this is not a test. You're doing a fine job, okay? It'll only take you a minute, and I promise I won't tell on you. I just really need to get rid of this headache."

"Oh, okay."

When Taylor left the office, Drummond clapped his hands. "Well, done. You're starting to get the knack of some of this job. A few days ago, you'd never have pulled of such an easy lie like that."

"I'm not lying. That witch of yours gave me a horrible headache."

"You saw her, then. Great! What did she say? What do we have to do?"

Max got out his laptop and powered up. "Taylor'll be back pretty fast and we can't have a non-stop phone conversation while he's here."

"That's true. You're not that great a liar, yet."

"But I can type out my answers here," he said, pointing to the laptop.

"Fine, fine. Now before that dimwit gets back, what did the witch say?"

"She said that you're under a binding spell."

"Gee, really? I could have told you that."

"Then why didn't you? From what Connor said, I gather you know a lot about witches and voodoo and all that nonsense. Why not just tell me what you need instead of sending me off into the night like that?"

Drummond stepped closer to Max like a father trying to explain the hard choices of parenting. "I'm sorry about that, but I didn't think you'd believe me otherwise. Even though you've handled this whole ghost business very well, and I'm proud of you about that — heck, most people would've packed up and moved home already — but now we're getting into something a little harder to swallow. Ghosts is one thing. Everybody has a haunting story in their lives — friends, family, or personal experience. There's enough evidence out there to bring in enough doubt that you can accept such a thing when it's in front of your eyes. But witches? Magic spells? That's a whole lot harder to accept."

"I suppose. I'm just sick of being everybody's pawn."

"Help me get free from this binding spell and I promise you, I'll do all I can to get you in a better position."

Taylor walked in carrying a paper bag. His eyes burst out at the sight of the laptop. "You-You-You can't do that in here. Please, Mr. Porter, put that away."

"Just give me the bag," Max said, his headache winding up again at the sight of relief.

As Taylor handed over the bag, he said, "You know you're not allowed to use that laptop in here. Please put it away. I promise I won't tell."

Max popped two capsules in his mouth and swallowed them dry. "No," he said, savoring the moment of defiance. "You can tell Modesto or whoever you want. Go ahead. Tell him I don't care about his stupid rules anymore."

Drummond nodded his approval. "You tell him."

With his face tightening, Taylor said in an odd and unnerving quiet, "Okay. If that's what you want. I'll just be over here." He walked to the wall opposite the bookshelf and sat on the floor.

Drummond laughed. "That's one troubled kid. Forget about him, Max. He'll be fine. Now, tell me what we've got to do. See there are lots of binding spells and I don't know this one at all. If I did, I wouldn't be stuck here still."

Max's attention lingered on Taylor. However, Drummond was right. There were more important things at hand. Max pulled the laptop closer, opened his word processor, and typed: CONNOR SAID THE MARKINGS ON THE FLOOR HAD TO BE COPIED IN A BOOK OR SCROLL OR SOMETHING.

"It was a book. I remember that."

WE HAVE TO FIND THAT BOOK AND DESTROY IT HERE.

"Okay. Does she have any idea where to find it?"

SHE MIGHT.

"But she wouldn't tell you, would she?"

SHE WANTS TO SPEAK WITH YOU.

"Crap."

WHAT HAPPENED? WHAT DID YOU DO TO HER?

"Nothing. Not to her, at least."

WHAT DOES THAT MEAN?

"There's got to be another way."

JUST TELL ME.

"I don't want to go into it. You need to find some other way. There's got to be."

The laptop beeped the arrival of an e-mail. Max opened the program and read the e-mail twice. ARE YOU READING THIS?

"Yeah," Drummond said. "Looks like Annabelle got all her stock as a gift."

LOOK HERE. IT WENT THROUGH FOUR DIFFERENT COMPANY NAMES BEFORE IT REACHES HER.

"We need to find out who owns those companies."

SOMETHING TELLS ME THE NAME HULL MIGHT COME UP.

"Congratulations. You've experienced your first hunch. Now do your book thing you're so good at and let's get some answers."

WHAT ABOUT YOU?

Drummond passed through one of Taylor's paper stacks and watched it fall over. "We'll do the best we can until you figure out another way to break this spell or where that book might be."

Taylor jumped to his feet and said in that same odd tone he had used before, "Gee, sir, I'm so sorry. I forgot to tell you that Mr. Modesto wanted to have breakfast with you at 10:30. I believe he said at Cities. I guess you'll be late."

"That little prick," Drummond said. Max closed his laptop and glared at Taylor. "Keep it cool, Max. We've got a lot of information on our side. Just go meet with Modesto and make him think we don't know anything."

Max nodded, grinned, and with as much control as he

could manage, he said, "That's okay, Taylor. Mistakes happen. Please be more mindful of my appointments in the future. You wouldn't want me to be late again. Mr. Modesto might ask for an explanation."

Without a further glance in Taylor's direction, Max grabbed his laptop and left the office.

Chapter 12

WHEN MAX ARRIVED AT CITIES, a restaurant not too far from Dr. Connor's office, Mr. Modesto had ordered for them both and offered a curt nod. He snapped his fingers toward the chair opposite him and waited for Max to sit. Though the gesture (too close to being treated like a dog) boiled in Max's heart, he remained quiet and did as commanded.

"I do not appreciate being kept waiting," Modesto said as he typed out a text message on his phone.

"I'm sorry. My new assistant made a mistake."

"So quick to blame others."

"No blame, just a mistake."

"Of course. In other matters, I trust you are settling in fine since I've not heard otherwise. Our employer wishes you to be as comfortable as possible. Also ..."

Modesto droned on, but Max only half-heard anything the man said. The briefcase stole Max's attention. He noticed it when he had arrived, leaning against the legs of Modesto's chair as if it could feel casual and relaxed. Inside, Max suspected, would be much of the information he wanted. It had to be there. Modesto handled Max for Hull which meant that Modesto would have all the papers pertaining to Max. Even if his hopes were misplaced and the briefcase did not contain crucial information, it still had to have something of use. All Max had to do was wait until the end of the meal when Modesto would to go to the bathroom like always.

"... Moravian government proved quite interesting," Modesto went on. "In fact, you've helped us fill in a few blanks we ..."

Even if Modesto went to the bathroom, could Max do it? He stared at that briefcase, trying to hold down the nerves bucking to get out, trying to keep his mind focused. If he got caught, if Modesto returned early — but no, he couldn't think in those terms. In order to rifle through that briefcase, Max forced himself to ignore all other concerns — one languishing moment of fear would stop him from doing what he now believed to be imperative.

"Excuse me a moment," Modesto said and left for the restrooms.

Just like that, Max's opportunity landed. He made no motions at first, caught unprepared. How long had he sat at that table while Modesto prattled away for them to reach this point in the meal? If not for the clicking of forks on plates, Max would have remained frozen until Modesto returned; however, he did hear that sound and it brought to mind a ticking clock.

Swallowing any guilt, Max slid the briefcase toward his chair (it was heavier than it appeared) and pulled a handful of papers out. The top ones carried the Hull corporation header and had been addressed to Modesto. A cursory glance showed they were daily orders with reference to "reports" made by his assistant. No surprises there.

The next was a letter dated the day before and read:

> Mr. Modesto —
> Your recent account of Max Porter's activities, particularly his unforeseen visit to

Dr. Connor, requires an acceleration of our timetable. While it would have been preferable to wait for Mr. Porter to conclude on his own that the location of Old Salem was most profitable to our interests, we can no longer afford such patience. Therefore, we ask that you steer him toward that locale.

Max re-read the letter, all the time feeling as if a hidden psychopath stalked his every move. He wanted to rush home and search for bugs, wire-taps, or whatever high-tech surveillance equipment he could find — not that he had a clue how to look for such things, but he could not idle on the idea that he was being watched. He considered reading the letter a third time but instead he pushed the papers back into the briefcase. Modesto would be returning any second. As Max attempted to get the papers to look untouched, the name *Drummond* flashed from one page, and Max turned his head to read it clearer. Laughter from another table brought him to his senses, yet even as he used his foot to slide the briefcase back into position, he caught the words *Broughton* and *Kirksbride Plan*.

"That's really all we have to discuss today," Modesto said as he stepped toward the table. Max put on his best attitude of nonchalance as Modesto lifted his briefcase onto the table and began looking through it. The paper with Drummond's name on it stuck a little higher than the others, and Max felt sure Modesto had seen it. However, the man did nothing but take out a hundred dollar bill and hand it to the waitress.

"I'll be leaving, now," Modesto said. Then, as if just recalling a little, unimportant thought, he added, "By the way, our employer feels you have proven yourself well. Your historical research was adequate and the initial land deals researched was fine. You have enough background to start seeking out the properties we may wish to acquire."

"Okay, great."

"Articulate as ever, I see. Regardless, you'll find it easiest to begin in the historic areas as they have some of the oldest land which I know to be of high value."

"The historic areas," Max said, hoping the sourness he heard in his voice could not be detected by Modesto. "Any suggestions?"

"If I knew the best way to handle this, your services would not be required, would they? But, if I must hazard my opinion on the matter, then I'd suggest considering Old Salem. It's the closest in the area. There are others as well, but I suppose that's a good place to start."

"Old Salem? I'll be sure to look into it."

"I'll let our employer know. I must go now."

Max sat alone for several minutes, listening to the restaurant bustle around him and waiting for his heart to stop racing. When he reached the point that he felt he could stand without an embarrassing stumble, he left the building and settled in his car. Again, he waited awhile, just letting the world slow down around him.

When he finally headed onto the road, his mind juggled one idea after another, trying to make sense of all the insanity that had occurred since his arrival in North Carolina. None of it added up to his liking (though he did admit that some things were coming together). The thought that hit him at least once each day now blared into his brain — *I should grab Sandra, sell the house, and leave this town.* But he knew he would not do it. First — Sandra loved it here, and he refused to ruin it for her like he had in Michigan. Second, and far more important if he was honest with himself — he wanted to solve these mysteries. A sliver inside him understood what drove men like Drummond, what drove many to read about men like Drummond, and what drove even more to watch television shows about men like Drummond. The puzzles had to have answers, and even though his life careened onward like a drunk driver passed out at the wheel, the puzzles could be solved. That's the allure. Solving the mystery gave him a little control in this world.

As he slowed down to pass a parked police car, he decided to put everything into some order. He had a lot of research to do: Old Salem, Hull, and now Broughton and Kirksbride. That alone could take days. The letter in Modesto's briefcase made it certain that Hull, Drummond, and this missing book to break the curse were all related, so his level of thoroughness would have to be extreme. However, his mind gravitated toward Annabelle Bowman.

Hers was the oddity in all this. What about her and her husband, Stan, connected to Drummond and Hull? Drummond said his investigation into Stan Bowman led to Hull. Maybe so. But how and why? Annabelle received a gift of R. J. Reynolds stock via dummy corporations that lead back to Hull. This stock made her millions. Why? What did Hull seek to buy with this money?

"Okay," Max said out loud. "The truth is I'm sick of the library." Research was one thing. Research trying to save your butt was another — a far more stressful way to work.

When his cell phone chirped, Max jumped. He growled at the car, and with shaking hands, he pulled to the roadside before he answered the phone. "Hello," he said, all civility absent.

"Mr. Porter?" a muffled voice asked, but it had a clear Southern drawl.

Max's nerves tightened even more. "Yes?"

"Please start driving your car."

Any threatening message, any bullying tone, would have

angered Max, but he would have managed. This, however, churned his stomach. With as nonchalant a maneuver as he could muster, Max tried to look around the area for a spy.

"Please, Mr. Porter," the voice said. "If you want the truth about Stan Bowman, pull onto the road."

Unsure what to do, Max did as ordered. "Who are you?"

"Take Route 40 East to Durham, then take 85 North."

"Durham? That's almost two hours from here."

"From 85 North, get off on Exit 189 for Butner. You understand?"

"Who is this?"

"Do you understand?"

Max repeated the directions.

"That's correct," the voice said and hung up.

Two hours provided Max with plenty of time to think and to worry. Even as the miles droned on and his conscience told him he was crazy to follow these directions blindly, his desire to get some bit of information overwhelmed all other concerns. He banished the idea that he might be in physical danger. Deep inside, he knew that to be true, but to give voice to such fears would only undermine his determination.

He thought about calling Sandra but decided against it. He didn't want to risk missing a call from his informant. *Informant?* Yes, the word fit. After all, the man had contacted him with a promise of "the truth about Stan Bowman."

When his cell phone rang, Max answered it before it finished its first chirp. "Hello?"

"When you come off the exit ramp, you'll see a red pickup truck. Follow it."

As instructed, Max took the exit for Butner and found a red, Toyota pickup waiting. It pulled onto the road and turned west. Max followed.

They headed into a rural area, taking enough turns that Max felt lost. At length, the pickup headed onto a dirt road, drove another mile, and pulled over. Max parked behind the truck and waited.

The truck's door opened and a gray-haired man stepped out. He wore a simple outfit of slacks, an off-white shirt, and black suspenders. A slight bend and a grisly white beard added to his soft image. Any fears Max harbored vanished.

The old man waved to Max and pointed toward the hill across the road. Then he walked in that direction, shuffling his feet in slow but steady steps. Max got out of his car, stretched, and followed.

"Mr. Porter," the man said, offering his hand and a shining smile. "I apologize for the cloak-and-dagger bit. I can get a little paranoid. Then again, when you're dealing with the Hull family, a little paranoia ain't such a bad thing. Oh, sorry, my name's Phillip King."

"Pleasure to meet you."

King chuckled. "You sound awful wary. That's good. You should be. This is wary business."

"I don't mean to be rude, Mr. King, but this has turned into a long day already. You said you have information about Stan Bowman. For that matter, how'd you even know I was interested? Who are you?"

"Calm down," King said, and Max took a deep breath — he had not been aware of raising his voice and clenching his fists. "Now, let's see. I know about you because you upset Annabelle Bowman, and while Winston-Salem has become a decent-sized city, many parts of it are still very small town. Word gets around. Especially about old sore spots like Stan. As for me, well I used to work for Reynolds Tobacco. In fact, I worked in the factory where the POWs worked, where Stan Bowman took seven of them and turned them into nutcases."

"You were there?"

"I know all about it."

"Then I'm very interested," Max said, staring at the open grass dotted with sparse trees. "Was it really necessary to come all the way out here?"

"It starts here. This field was where the POW camp was. One of eighteen in North Carolina. There was even one in the Winston-Salem area, but those fellas that Stan went after, they came from here."

"Can I write this down?" Max asked, itching to run back to his car and grab a notebook.

"You just listen. You'll remember enough."

"I wouldn't show anybody. I promise."

"No, Mr. Porter. We're going to do this my way."

"Okay. Your way."

"Now, it's like this: I first met Stan Bowman in 1944. He came back from the War with a bullet in his leg — made the thing near-useless. They gave him a medal, too. I hadn't been able to go because I couldn't pass the physical. I've got a bad hip. So, I'll admit I was jealous of him. I could see the way the ladies gave him an extra few seconds with their eyes, the way they seemed ready to break all their vows just for a night with an acknowledged hero or something like that. Point is, I was jealous, and so I took it upon myself to befriend the man. I suppose I thought that by being close to him, I might get something of what he had, but that's an old man talking. Truth is, at the time, I just did what I did. Didn't give it that much thought.

"Stan took a job driving trucks, so I saw him every week when he hauled tobacco in from the farms for processing. It was hard work for everybody but Reynolds took good care of us. Heck, we'd all have been without jobs if it weren't for him. The entire town of Winston-Salem owes that family their lives.

"Anyway, we'd go out every night with a handful of girls and a lot of beer. Every night. It was exhausting fun," King said, blushing and laughing at the same time. "Went on like that for quite awhile. Maybe even a month, though I'm probably bragging. Still, it seemed that long. Until he met Annabelle and the parties stopped.

"The day comes we get word that a bunch of German POWs were coming. Reynolds had finagled a deal to get free labor from them, and the government hoped if we treated them well, the Germans would treat our boys that were prisoners well, too. There were some awful stories coming back but nothing like what we'd eventually find out. By that time, Stan and Annabelle were full on in love and talking about marriage. I suppose it would have happened all like a fairy tale for them if Hull hadn't shown up."

"You met Hull?"

"Yup, I met him. William Hull. His boy Terrance probably runs the whole thing now. If not, he will someday soon, but back then, William strutted around like he was the greatest man in the world. I don't think Reynolds liked him too much. At least, that was the gossip."

"When did you meet him? What happened?"

"I'm getting there. Just let me tell you. Now, I only met the man once. Reynolds was showing him the factory, answering questions about POWs and all that. I suppose Hull was thinking about making his own deal with the government. Reynolds called me over and introduced me. I ain't nothing special, don't mistake me. Reynolds called me over so Hull could hear what it was like from the common man. Could've been anybody but he called over me.

"Hull was a tall fellow with the sternest face I'd ever seen. I mean this man stared down at me like I was a threat to his family and he was prepared to kill me with his bare hands if it came to it. I'm not exaggerating. He shook my hand and stared at me and I'll tell you, I was a bit scared. Never had that happen before or since — that I got scared just from the look in a man's eyes. It was odd, but not nearly as odd as what happened next."

"Wait a minute," Max said, closing his eyes and painting an image of this moment in his head. He knew he would never remember all the details but hoped that a simple snapshot in his brain might help out more than trying to recall King's every word. With a nod, he said, "Okay, what happened next that was so odd?"

"Reynolds calls up some of the POWs and has them line up in front of Hull. Hull paces up and down the line like he's Patton or something. He looked more like a fool than anything else but I just worked steady and peeked at the goings on from the corner of my eye. Now, here's the odd part.

"On his second pass, he's coming in my direction so I can see his hard face clear as day, and he hesitates for the tiniest moment and I swear his face dropped. I mean, he recognized one of them POWs. I have no doubt in my mind about it. That little pause lasted a long time in my mind and I know what I saw. I'm not saying Hull was in cahoots with the Germans, but he certainly knew something about that one in particular."

King stopped speaking and looked upon the empty field that once housed the enemies of the United States with his eyes sparkling in satisfaction. He stood straighter, and Max recognized a man lifted of his burden. For Max, though, the burdens continued to pile on and many could not be seen. Every one of King's freeing breaths inflated disbelief in Max.

"That's it?" Max said. "You brought me all the way out here to tell me that Hull might have, maybe, possibly, known a Nazi or two?"

With a patronizing pat on the shoulder, King said, "You're not listening too well. Hull, who never before and never after, steps foot into our factory, sees a prisoner who he is, in some way, knowledgeable of, and then just a few days later, Stan Bowman, a man who has plenty of good going for him, a stable man with a beautiful woman at his side — well, he goes crazy and kidnaps seven of these prisoners. That seems like a big coincidence to me. Not enough for you? The reason I brought you here is because all seven of those men — one of which was the man I saw Hull recognize — all seven of them came from this camp here in Butner. All the rest of the prisoners who labored in our factory came from the Winston-Salem camp. But these seven are driven hours out of the way to come work at a place that ultimately leads to their torture and madness. Is that really just a coincidence?"

"There was an investigation," Max said, trying to act more like a detective and not an excited amateur. "Why didn't you bring any of this up back then?"

"You think I was going to go up against a man like Hull? I had a life I was building. I didn't want to throw that away over a bunch of Krauts."

"Then why now? You just old enough that you don't care anymore?"

"A little bit, perhaps. Or perhaps I'm tired of sleepless nights, knowing that I failed to do the right thing. Perhaps I see a young man and his beautiful wife lured down here to become mired way over their heads in an old Southern bog, and I see a chance for a little redemption. Doesn't really matter, though, does it? Not to you. You've got what I know now, and I don't ever want to see you again."

"But why did —"

"No more, Mr. Porter. It's time for you to go," King

said and crouched in the grass.

Max did not move at first. Too late, the idea dawned that he should have asked if Hull carried a book. He opened his mouth but said nothing. The old man's determined concentration on the empty hills formed a steel wall against further talk. Max didn't even bother with saying *Thank you.*

Before driving away, he pulled out a pad and pen and jotted down every bit he could recall. Detective work had proven to be more taxing than he had expected. All these threads had to be kept in order so that he remembered the questions at the important times. Already, he could hear Drummond complaining about his missed opportunity regarding the book. At least, he had more on the Bowman case.

With so much time to get through until he reached home, he planned to think about all he had learned. However, his head pounded and he found a soothing jazz station to clear his mind from any thoughts. Miles drifted by without his awareness. As his headache eased away, two loud snaps startled him and the car swerved off the road.

Max wrenched the steering wheel to the left but the car barreled forward. The steering wheel shivered in his hands. Gravel peppered the undercarriage like a snare drum. The backend of the car kept turning, turning, and Max had time to think the car might flip if it turned anymore. He let the wheel roll back in the opposite direction, trying not to fishtail. Braking at the same time as he fought the car, he managed to slow down. At length, he stopped. Sweat stung his eyes and his fingers danced on every surface they touched.

He took several minutes to focus on little more than breathing. Cars passed by with gawking faces peering from inside like caricatures at an amusement park. All of life slowed down until he regained enough sense to move.

He stepped from the car and inspected the front right wheel. Little of it was left. Max did not bother getting the donut from the trunk — he had no doubt in his mind the tiny emergency tire had no air in it. Instead, he called for a tow truck. Before he heard the second ring on the phone, he saw a small hole in the car's frame just above the shredded tire — no rust around the hole, and the metal bent toward the wheel as if something had shoved through from the outside.

"Like a bullet," he whispered, recalling the snaps right before he lost control of the car.

After arranging for the tow truck, and being told to wait inside his car, Max paced around, checking for more bullet holes. Somebody had shot at him, and he didn't know what to feel — it had never happened before. He kicked the car and screamed at the sky and spit on the ground. Huffing and red-faced, he opened the car door and sat facing the road with his head in his hands.

Too late to go back now. Not that he could ever go back to Michigan. The people up there were always good to him, but he knew them well — they would not forget. *Probably true down here, too.* That was the real problem. No matter where he could run, Hull would not leave him alone. Besides, Max agreed with Sandra. The only way beyond this was to go straight through.

"So, where am I?" he said, arching his back and tasting the salty trickles of sweat on his lips. "Okay, the best I can see is that near the end of World War II, R. J. Reynolds makes his POW deal and starts using them in Winston-Salem. For some reason, Hull visits this factory and recognizes seven of them. Why does he want them dead? Does it matter? Anyway, I don't know, but he gets Stan Bowman to do it and then pays off Annabelle with stock to keep her quiet."

Only the whisk of passing cars responded.

It would take another hour-and-a-half before his car had been towed and a new tire installed. A few more hours drive, and Max made it home. The day had ended.

Except for the phone call.

Before Max had removed his coat, the phone rang. He answered it, clamping down on his desire to bark out a few rude remarks, with a simple, "Yes?"

A deep voice said, "Last warning, Porter. Next time we won't be shooting at the tires." The phone went dead.

Max slammed the phone down and tore off his coat. "Fuckers," he spat out. Then he grabbed the phone and punched in a number he knew too well.

"Hello, Mr. Porter," Modesto said.

"What the hell is the matter with you people?" Max said, his voice rising as he stormed around his living room.

"Calm down, please."

"Fuck you. You send your muscle to threaten me and my wife, and now you're shooting at me? I'm doing everything you've asked of me. I'm working as fast as I can."

"Shooting? Somebody shot at you?"

"Don't even start with that crap."

"Mr. Porter, I assure you we are not the cause of this. Now calm down and explain to me what happened."

"You know what happened," Max said, but he doubted himself now. Modesto sounded truly surprised by the call.

"Please, take a moment to think this through. What good could possibly come from our employer attacking you? As you pointed out, you're doing a fine job for us. Why would he spend all this money and effort to bring you down to North Carolina and put you to work, if he simply wanted to kill you? It makes no sense, does it?"

Max flopped onto his couch. "No."

"Now what happened?"

In a few minutes, Max laid out the events of the shooting. He avoided any mention of Phillip King, Butner, Bowman, and World War II POWs. The shooting itself was sensational enough to make omissions easy.

"Thank you," Modesto said. "I think I understand quite clearly now."

"So, what do we do?"

"You just go back to your job. I'll handle this."

"I want to know who did this. I want them to be put behind bars."

"I will find out who is responsible, and you can rest knowing that I will make sure they are taken care of."

Max straightened. "Wait a minute. No, no. I'm not saying I want that. Just get them arrested."

"I don't know what you mean by 'that' but don't worry."

"You know exactly what I mean. Don't kill them," Max said, whispering the last two words.

"Good-bye, Mr. Porter," Modesto said and hung up. Max looked at the phone as if he had no clue how it had managed to get in his hand.

"What was that?" Sandra asked.

Max dropped the phone as he jumped. His eyes darted toward her. "Honey, I didn't mean to wake you up."

Sandra stood in the bedroom doorway, her arms crossed, all sensuousness missing despite her negligee. "Who were you talking to?"

"What? Oh, just Modesto."

"Just? Are you going to tell me that I misunderstood? That you didn't talk to him about killing people? Are you?" Angry as she was, Max could see her desperate hope that he would tell her just that — she had misunderstood.

"Come here. Sit down."

Tears welled in her eyes. "What's happening here? Please, tell me you didn't ... please."

Max waited for Sandra to sit next to him on the couch. He held her hands, and said, "I was shot at tonight."

"Shot?"

"I'm fine. I was just angry. That's all you heard. And I didn't tell him to kill anybody. I told him *not* to. I just want them caught and put in jail. Honest."

"Honest?"

"You know me. I wouldn't try to kill somebody."

"I know."

"It scares me that you'd think that."

Sandra pulled back. "It scares *you?* What am I suppose to think? You've been acting weird ever since that Drummond stuff started. I know there's a lot of pressure on you, and I know this is a tough situation, but still — you don't even call to say where you are, when you'll be home, or anything. I've barely seen you the last few days. And these people — I mean, your employer is powerful. I think that much is clear. And powerful people can be very persuasive. Power can be very alluring. I worry."

"Honey, look at me. I'm one of the good guys."

As Sandra's tears fell, she wrapped her arms around Max and kissed him. He held her tight, pressing his lips hard against hers, his body acknowledging that they had not made love in far too long. Heat washed between them like water cascading across their limbs. Both struggled for breath but neither let go of the embrace.

Max's kissing moved to Sandra's neck and she let out a soft groan. He pulled back and held her face. "I'm scared," he said. "I want to run away from here but we can't."

"I know," she said, kissing him and unbuttoning his shirt. "I know. I'm scared, too. When you don't call, I worry you might be —"

"I'm here. I'm fine." He pressed his body against hers.

Max kicked off his pants and eased inside Sandra. They both let out moans of pleasure mixed with relief. Then they giggled at their own sounds.

"See," Max said, "we're fine."

Sandra rocked her hips back and forth. "That's because you're the good guy."

"That's right. Very right."

Making love erased the world around them. Max gave in without protest. He felt a bit disoriented when, late in the evening, he sat on the couch flipping through television channels. Sandra's head rested in his lap, her soft snores a gentle reminder of how pleasant life could be when given the opportunity.

Max stopped at Channel 12 local news and listened to tomorrow's forecast (cloudy and sixty-five). The anchor came back on and pictures of four men appeared. Two were tattooed thugs who looked as if a few years in prison would be a vacation. The third man, a crew-cut blonde with a tight face and hateful eyes, looked to be the brains among the four. Either that or he would be playing the girl during his prison stay. The last man, a heavyset man — Max recognized him. Max would never forget him — he could still smell the man's reek as he punched Max in the gut.

Max turned up the volume. "... were arrested today on charges of racketeering following an anonymous tip ..."

He hit the MUTE button and gaped at the television. *An anonymous tip.* Modesto? Could it all be over? And if so, then what does it mean that in a matter of hours, Modesto had managed this? Max felt both filthy and relaxed. He had four men arrested with just a phone call.

"Am I the good guy?" he asked. Sandra's soft snores were his only answer.

Chapter 13

AFTER A BREAKFAST OF EGGS AND TOAST smothered in kisses, cranberry juice with a flash of skin, and a glass of water with dessert upstairs, Max extracted himself from Sandra's arms and drove to his office. Their morning together helped keep him from reviewing the disturbing events of the previous night. As far as he cared to recall, the night was filled with making love. What had led up to it needed no analysis — at least, not for the moment.

"Good morning, Mr. Porter," Taylor said.

Max strode by the young man and powered up his laptop. Drummond poked his head from the bookcase, winked at Max, and floated closer.

"Thought I heard you," he said. "Any developments overnight? Any closer to finding that book?"

Once the laptop was ready, Max typed out a quick detail of his meeting with Phillip King and then being shot at. As Drummond thought, he passed through Taylor several times. Max suspected this to be more malice than accident but grinned nonetheless. Before Drummond could ask again, Max typed I'VE GOT NO INFORMATION ON THE BOOK YET.

"As long as you're trying. I've been stuck here for a long time. What's a few more days?"

ASSUMING I FIND IT.

"You'll find it," Drummond said, his façade of confidence unable to mask his nerves. "Tell me, did you get a name for the POW?"

IT WAS YOUR CASE. DON'T YOU KNOW IT?

"That was over a half-century ago. You expect me to remember every little detail? Check the police report, it should be in there."

Max pulled up the file and skimmed over it.

JOSEPH RICHTER?

"That's one of them. Also Günther something. You need to check on those today."

I WILL. BUT I ALSO NEED YOU TO TELL ME SOMETHING.

"What do you want to know?"

WHY IS YOUR NAME CONNECTED WITH BROUGHTON AND THE KIRKSBRIDE PLAN?

Drummond halted.

I CAN DO THE RESEARCH RIGHT HERE, BUT YOU'LL SAVE ME A LOT OF TIME, Max typed. Drummond said nothing, so Max pulled up his internet browser and searched Broughton. As the listing came up, including the heading WEST CAROLINA INSANE ASYLUM, Drummond said, "Stop that thing. Let me tell you before you get it all twisted up in your head. Just shut it off."

Max closed the browser, and Drummond sighed in relief. "Thank you," Drummond said. "Look, this is nothing like it appears there."

BROUGHTON ISN'T A MENTAL INSTITUTION?

"You know it is. You just saw it. But just hear me out, okay? I'm not crazy. Of all the people I've ever told this to, what I'm going to tell you, I think you might believe me. After all, you're sitting here listening to a ghost."

I'M WAITING.

"Okay, okay. Don't get all snooty with me," Drummond said. After a slight swipe through Taylor's head, he settled in front of Max and said, "Well, at first, I was a cop walking the beat, just getting started. I drank a little but not too much and even back then people said I had a knack for solving tough problems. Everybody thought I'd be a full-fledged detective in no time at all.

"One night, a blistering August night, I was done and on my way home when I heard an odd noise coming from a second-floor window. It had a mournful sound like a kitten crying 'cause its mom had died. I saw right away that it was Ms. Holstein's apartment — nice old lady who spent much of her time knitting by that window. I wasn't on duty anymore that night, but when you're a cop, you're never really off duty — not for a real cop. So, I went up to take a look.

"Before I reached the door, I knew Ms. Holstein was dead. That nasty Death-smell had already begun to seep into the hall. And then that sad sound cried out again. I knocked on the door. Said something stupid like 'Ms. Holstein? Are you okay in there?' but of course, I got no answer. I tried the door and found it unlocked. Now at this point, I should have — I don't know anymore, really. Maybe it all was inevitable."

Max watched Drummond fidgeting and felt the sudden urge to pat the detective's shoulder. He couldn't, of course, but the urge grew anyway. The way Drummond had said *inevitable* struck Max with a sense of recognition — he, too, felt much of what had been happening to him was beyond his control. Perhaps, even though he loathed the idea of destiny, perhaps *inevitable*.

"Well, I went into that apartment," Drummond continued, "and I found Ms. Holstein face down by the window. No blood or signs of struggle. It looked like she just finally died and that was that. Then I heard that crying again. I turned around and standing by the bedroom door was Ms. Holstein — only she was shimmering. I guess I don't have to tell you what I'm talking about, do I?"

"You saw her ghost," Max said.

Taylor startled from his book. "What was that, sir?"

"Nothing. Forget it."

Taylor eyed Max for a moment before returning to his book. Drummond tsked. "That boy really should get another job. Anyway, yeah, I saw her ghost and it scared the hell out of me. I probably looked like an imbecile standing there with my mouth open, but I couldn't move. I just kept thinking that it didn't make any sense. I don't know how long I stood there waiting for something to happen, maybe my own death — I don't really know. Eventually, she vanished but slowly. More like she dissipated. Anyway, she was gone.

"To prove how much of an idiot I was back then, I opened my big mouth and wrote up the whole incident in my report. The week wasn't over before I'd been canned.

"The Depression was on, so losing my job was serious. I was lucky, though — no wife, no kids, nothing but myself to cost me a dime. So I rented out this office and became a private detective. The landlord knew I was using it as an apartment as well, but he was a good man and I paid my rent which was more than many people did, so he let me stay."

Drummond took in the little office with a reminiscent gleam. "Anyway," he said, "I did a few jobs here and there, just enough to keep me afloat, but I couldn't stop thinking about that ghost. So one night after I had a whiskey or two too many, I went back to that old place. Nobody had moved in — or at least, nobody had stayed long. I walked inside being cautious and sure that nothing would happen, but there she was standing by the door as if no time had gone since she last saw me. This time she pointed to the wall. It took me forever to move my body, but in the end, I found what she wanted. Hidden in the wall was a box full of cash and a note that she had saved it for her niece. I delivered the cash, almost two hundred dollars, and before you even ask, the answer is no, I didn't take a nickel. Heck, I didn't dare. And that was it for the ghost. She was gone.

"I'll tell you something. If it had ended there, I would've been happier than if I had been Marilyn Monroe's pillow. But a few weeks later, in walks this gorgeous dame, says she needs some help with a delicate situation. I'm thinking it's adultery but it turns out something else entirely. She says she's a witch and she's ticked off some evil spirits. I wanted to think she'd lost it, but I knew about ghosts now, why not witches? And before you ask, yes, she was Connor's grandmother. After that case, word spread that I was the go-to-guy for the weird and spooky. Four cases later and I started looking for a 'special' kind of vacation. When I found out about the whole Kirksbride thing, I checked myself into the asylum."

WHAT'S KIRKSBRIDE? Max typed.

"Well, you know, asylums weren't the nicest places to be, even back then. It wasn't the dark ages or anything, and it certainly wasn't England, but it was an ugly business. Except this Kirksbride character. He had this idea of making a peaceful, open place where one could rest his mind and deal with his troubles. It wasn't a prison guarded by sadists. They offered real help. And by that point, after all the things I'd seen, I was close to losing my mind. I was desperate for help. And that's that. Now you know why I was there. This is a bizarre world we live in, and I just needed a little help in finding a way to cope with it."

BUT THE ASYLUM DOCTORS DIDN'T BELIEVE

YOU, DID THEY?

"Of course not. But that didn't matter. Being there, seeing people who had truly lost their minds, helped put everything in perspective. I mean that's a big part of handling life. You have to maintain perspective. You have to realize that all the decisions you make don't really add up to all that much. You're not going to stop the Earth from moving or the Sun from burning. So just relax."

Drummond made it sound simple, but Max did not subscribe to the notion with ease. For him, echoes of the previous night bounced in his head. How could he "just relax" when people had shot at him, when a move to the South to fix his troubled life had only made it worse, or when his own actions may have sent men to prison? Granted, they belonged in prison, but nothing he could reason made him feel any better because in the end, it didn't matter that the thugs were in jail. They were just hired hands. Whoever wanted to hurt Max was still out there.

The rest of the day, Max buried himself in research. He stole his WiFi access from somebody nearby so he wouldn't have to leave the office. Twice Taylor asked if Max would be going out, and twice Taylor fumbled his reaction when Max said he would be staying in.

The research did not go well. He found out the basics about Old Salem — the historic area that comprised some of Salem's original buildings and had now become an attraction with actors portraying the city's early settlers. Before long, however, he scoured the local newspaper websites for reports on the arrests. Upon locating two articles, he read them several times. Except for one bit of information, the articles had little to say. That one bit, though, made up for a lot: the names of the four men — Wilson McCoy, Edward Moore, Chad Barrows, and Cole

Eckerd.

The names settled around Max's head like taunting devils — one on each shoulder, one at each ear. These little pieces of evil did not try to tempt him, however. Instead, they threatened him and Sandra over and over. He could hear them saying he should back away before something bad happened.

By the time Taylor gave a weak good-bye and left with his head hanging and his hands stuffed in his pockets, Max had not thought of anything else but those men for hours. The sun had set. Drummond watched Taylor leave and then clapped his hands. "Okay, now we can get to work," he said, settling in the chair opposite Max.

"And do what? Get my house blown up?"

"Look, fella, I'm not thrilled to hear you're seeing the ugly side of this business but that doesn't change a damn thing. You get shot at sometimes. You learn to live with it."

"I don't want to live with it."

Drummond laced his hands behind his head. "Then go."

Max didn't bother with an answer. He delved into more online research and ignored the impatient ghost mulling about the office. He found an article about the POWs that had one interesting point — several politicians were suspected of taking bribes because of the unnecessary and unwanted seven POWs from Butner. No names, though. No pictures.

About an hour later, a man with white hair ringing a bald head knocked on the door. "Come in," Max said and gestured to the chair.

The man stepped in, his eyes surveying the office, and with an astounded smile, he said, "Nothing's changed."

"Can I help you?"

"I don't know. My name is Samuel Stevenson and I was good friends with Marshall Drummond."

Chapter 14

MAX NARROWED HIS EYES UPON SAMUEL STEVENSON, not out of a desire to intimidate but because Max knew that if he allowed himself one moment to breathe, his eyes would dart to the back corner of the room where Drummond, with his chest puffed in triumph, leaned against the wall. Stevenson gazed at the ceiling, then the bookcase, and finally onto the floor. When he saw the markings, he clicked his tongue.

"I always said Drummond would go out 'cause of something like this."

Drummond laughed. "That's true. All my weird cases gave Sam the willies."

Max gestured to the chair once more. "Mr. Stevenson, please have a seat."

Stevenson walked toward the books and began mouthing the titles. Drummond came closer and said, "Don't take offense. Sam here has had quite a nerve-wracking day."

"What did you do?" Max said before he could stop himself.

Sam faced Max. "For Drummond? Never anything official, but I helped out whenever I could."

"He was a cop," Drummond said.

"I see," Max said. "You were with the police?"

With a hesitant nod, Sam descended to his chair. Max thought the man might just hover an inch above the seat, afraid to commit to the act of sitting, but at length, Sam sat. His eyes jittered around the room.

"I can't believe this place," Sam said.

"It is rather a bit of time traveling. So, Mr. Stevenson, what can I do for you?"

Sam shook his head. "I'm here to help you."

"Me?" Max said, finally casting his gaze toward Drummond.

Drummond returned a proud smile and said, "You didn't think I'd just sit around and do nothing. I spent the last twenty-four hours working at getting my voice through the phone."

Max had to focus all his energy not to jump to his feet yelling about the irresponsible nature and uncaring attitude his ghost-partner exhibited. He frowned and said to Sam, "I don't follow you. How can you help me?"

"I see that look," Sam said. "I understand what you see in front of you."

"You do?"

"Sure. I'm an old man whose lost his marbles and is living in days gone by. Something like that I imagine. But you've got to trust me. I am sane. I think. It's just that I've seen something, that is, I've heard something that ... well, I don't know what to say to you. Good heavens, I sound crazier now than when I walked in here."

As Sam rubbed his face, Max looked at Drummond and asked, "What happened?"

Sam shuddered. "I don't know if I can explain."

"Look, I called the fellow, okay?" Drummond said. "I don't know how much he heard, but clearly something made it through. Now, listen to him because you need his help."

Sam cleared his throat, coughing phlegm into a handkerchief, and took a cleansing breath. "This is not going very well, is it?"

Max chuckled. "Let me help you out a bit. Did something strange happen to you? A voice, perhaps, or you saw something that might have been ghostlike?"

Sam's eyes widened but Max could not tell if this was a reaction of fear or astonishment. Then Sam broke into an old man's cackle. "I should've known," he said. "Marshall always was involved with the weird cases. Why should I be surprised to hear his dead voice? I mean, after all, I've seen some mighty oddball things working with him." For a few seconds, Sam's expression grew cold as his gaze drifted into memories. Then he said, "But how are you involved with Marshall?"

"This *was* his office."

"I guess his weird world stays close to home."

"I suppose. So, how exactly are you going to help me?"

"I don't really know."

Drummond stepped forward. "I figured he might still have access to information you can't get on your own. Ask him to look into the names you found of those morons who shot at you."

Max offered the task, and Sam brightened. "That's perfect. I still have a few old friends that could help us out. And, well, maybe that'll ease Marshall's spirit. Do you think? I mean, I know it's just Marshall — I hope — but having a dead man whisper to you over the phone ... look, at my age, I can't handle that."

"I understand," Max said. "I'm sure he'll leave you alone after this."

Drummond clapped his hands. "Don't bet on it," he said.

With the eagerness of a young man, Sam left the office,

still talking. "I'm on this right now. I'll call the moment I have anything helpful. Don't worry about it. You hear that Marshall? I'm helping out your friend."

Max pointed at Drummond and said, "How could you do that to a good friend?"

"Who? Sam? Do you have any idea how many times I saved his job? He'd have been a bum in the streets if it weren't for me. He owes me."

"You could've caused the old guy a heart attack."

"If having him help you gets me out of this curse, then I'll risk his ticker. Now, enough of that. Let's find this book already."

"No," Max said, his cheeks heating up.

"No?"

"Before I do anymore of this for you, I want you to promise you won't pull another thing like that, like what you did to Sam. You promise me that."

"You needed help."

"I need to know that you're not going to go haunting people. If Sam had a heart attack, if he died, then we'd have been responsible."

"So what? I'm already dead."

"I'm not," Max yelled.

Drummond rolled his eyes. "Okay, okay. I promise I won't haunt people to help us out."

With two raps on the door, Sandra walked in. "Knock, knock," she said.

"Honey?" Max rushed over to greet her, his mind racing for an excuse if she heard any of his argument with Drummond.

Sandra looked around the room before placing a wonderful smelling bag on the desk. "I brought dinner."

"How sweet."

"Well, with all you've been dealing with, I haven't seen

you much. Besides, last night —"

Max hugged her. "Thanks, hon."

"Hey," Drummond said. "Don't stop her. I want to hear about last night."

Sandra shot a nasty look in Drummond's direction. As Max pulled out the fried chicken dinner, Drummond moved closer and said, "Um, I think she can see me, Max."

Max and Sandra traded stunned eyes and both said, "What? You can see him?"

Chapter 15

OVER THE NEXT FEW HOURS, Max and Drummond listened as Sandra told them of her long history with the dead. It began at the age of thirteen when she saw the ghost of a neighbor shortly after the neighbor's wake. From then on, it never stopped. She spoke with the dead sometimes. Mostly she ignored them.

She glossed over much of her story, and Max did not press her for details. Her unusual shy behavior as she spoke told him to back off. Besides, he had enough imagination to paint in the missing parts — he saw the struggle she endured, the attempt to blot it out through destructive behavior, and finally, the acceptance of her ability. And after awhile, it became a regular part of her life.

She said that the ghosts never asked for her help or bothered her. Once in awhile they interrupted her during private moments in her life (like her honeymoon night), and she had to learn to live with the intrusions. Sometimes she found ghosts surprised she could talk to them, but usually they were too caught up in their own worlds to notice a living being — which was fine by her.

She never told anybody about her ability. Once, when visiting a psychic with her girlfriends, she thought she would be exposed. The psychic clearly sensed something odd about her, but he never gave her away — looking back,

Sandra often dismissed the whole thing as a coincidence brought on by a clever actor. "The only time I ever truly considered telling somebody was when you asked me to marry you," she said. "But things were so happy for us and I figured no good could possibly come from it. And I was frightened that you might react badly to the whole thing."

"Well, I'm angry. And hurt. You didn't trust me, and here I am trying to get things back the way they were, but now that's not even what I thought it was."

"I know. I'm sorry."

"Don't be. I'm upset, but that's just a gut, of-the-moment reaction. The fact is I'm just as guilty."

He proceeded to explain all about Drummond and the curse and Hull and everything regarding their predicament he had held back before. The words gushed out and relief followed. Even as he spoke, he thought about what her world must have been like — living a duplicitous life like a covert spy only she never saved the world, she only fought for a normal routine.

When he finished his story, he held her arms and said, "Look at that — we didn't explode. We told the truth and we're still here."

Drummond yawned. "I'm still here, too."

Sandra cracked a grin but stayed focused on Max. "There's hope for us yet."

"You know it," Max said. "From now on, no more secrets between us, okay?"

"Okay."

"Is there anything else I should know?"

Sandra steeled her expression before shaking her head. Then she said, "It looks like you boys could use my help."

Drummond jumped so fast he flew through his chair. "Wait just a minute here, young lady. You two can be lovebirds, but this part isn't a game. And it isn't some club you join. This is serious work."

"Marshall, may I call you Marshall?"

"No."

"Call him Drummond," Max said with a chuckle.

"Well then, Drummond, this isn't 1940 anymore."

"I'm aware of that," Drummond said as he flew about the room. "But the people we're dealing with are dangerous."

"Which is why you need me."

"I appreciate that you're Max's wife and that you can see me. But none of that —"

"Have you found your book yet?"

That stopped Drummond. He cast a suspicious eye towards Max. Max shook his head and said, "Calm down. She's on our side."

Sandra stepped closer to Max. "When I started seeing ghosts, especially during my teen years, I spent some time looking into the occult and witchcraft and all of that. I know a lot about what you're dealing with."

"Then enlighten us," Drummond said.

"If you agree to let me help."

Though a pale ghost, Drummond appeared to redden. Before he said a word, Max intervened. "Of course you can help. Whether Casper here wants to admit it or not, we need you. Now, what do you know about the book?"

"I know that it's not something most people would be comfortable keeping. When you bind a ghost, there's the object bound to and there's the holder. In this case, the object would be the page the spell was written on. The holder is the book, and holders tend to radiate energy." As Sandra delved into the finer points of binding spells, Max watched with an awe he had not experienced since he first fell for her. Little lines on her face filled him with excitement. He wanted to kiss her, to let her know that he loved her, to see her understand that all the ups and downs of the past months were coming to an end. Part of him, however, fought back — he feared the worst had yet to happen. It was a dark sensation reminding him of sitting in that witch's office.

"The witch," he blurted out.

"What?" Sandra asked.

Drummond swooped down. "Yes, yes. The witch."

Max said, "She hates you."

"I don't know if 'hate' is the right word."

Max said to Sandra, "There's a witch here in Winston-Salem. Her grandmother knew Drummond. They had a past. Well, not the best of past experiences together."

"You think she has the book?"

"She certainly didn't want to help him out. She told me only what I already knew and insisted on Drummond's apology."

"It sounds like a good place to start."

Max got to his feet, looked out the window as he thought, and then turned back to the others. "Why did you send me to her? No, no, don't give me that crap you said before. It just hit me now — you knew Connor's grandmother. Why would you send me to see this witch when you knew she would be angry?"

"I wasn't sure whose side she was on. We needed that information and you needed to learn about witches. I figured two birds one stone."

Before Max let loose a torrent of cursing, Sandra said, "It doesn't really matter, does it? You can't undo it."

"Listen to the lady," Drummond said.

"And now you know just how little you can trust this ghost."

"Don't listen to that part."

"We've got to deal with this witch, okay?" she said. Max

closed his eyes and nodded.

"Great," Drummond said. "So, she works out of an office. Max knows the place. You two could go in after hours."

"Break in?" Max said.

Sandra nodded. "Good idea. We should go tonight."

"Are you crazy? We can't break in."

"Why not?"

"How about jail for starters."

Drummond slid behind Sandra and shared a devilish grin. "Max," he said, "do we really need to put everything in perspective for you?"

"I know, I know," Max said.

"Well, that went easy. You know, Max, even though she doesn't trust me, I think I like your wife."

Sandra looked over her shoulder. "Thank you."

"If you two can tone it down, I'd like to know a few important details. For example, how are we going to break-in? Unless you're going to tell me you were a thief when you were a teen, honey, neither of us knows how to pick locks."

"I can do it," Drummond said, but when the other two stared at him, he added, "Well, I can."

"You'll have to teach me someday. For now, the break-in is off. We'll just have to think of another way to find that book." Max tried not to sound too relieved.

Drummond frowned. He moved his head from side to side, mouthing a debate that only he could hear. A few seconds later, he let out a loud sigh and said, "You won't have any trouble breaking-in because you won't have to. The doors will be unlocked. There's no security system or anything like that to worry about. Okay?"

"And you didn't want to mention this because?"

Drummond turned away and mumbled something.

Sandra said, "He wants to come with us, to be useful, but he keeps having to face the fact that he can't leave here."

"Oh," Max said, searching for something to change the subject with. He brightened as he latched onto the first thing to come to mind. "She knew I was coming before. She'll know we're coming again. She must be able to see the future."

"See the future? What kind of bozo are you?" Drummond said with a scowl. "Look, she doesn't live in a vacuum. I'm sure she has all sorts of sources of information spying all over to help her manipulate people."

"So, she's not a real witch?"

"Of course, she's real. Look what she did to me. It's just that no matter how much she tries to make people believe it, she can't see into the future. As far as I know."

"You're a bundle of confidence," Max said. A new thought struck, and he snapped his fingers. "Why will the doors be unlocked?"

Drummond turned back but stared at the floor. "Because Dr. Connor is a witch. Nobody would dare try to break into her office. Even those who don't know she's a witch sense she holds a lot of power because in all the years she's been in that little place, she has never once had any kind of trouble."

"Was that supposed to convince me?"

"You have to go, so just do it," Drummond said with a harshness that took Max by surprise. Then, in a softer tone, he said, "Please. I need you to do this."

Max closed his eyes. "Don't worry. If she has information that will help us, then I'll find it. I promise."

"Just go do what needs to be done. The rest is nothing to me. I just want a little freedom."

"Then we'll go to the office. We'll go right now."

Sandra winked at Max. "Guess we're back on," she said.

Twenty minutes later, Max sat in his car with Sandra next to him, waiting for the witch to leave her office. They parked in the lot across the street next to a dentist's office. While rain pelted the car and chilled the night, Max lost himself in the office sign's colors reflecting upon the pavement puddles. Neither Max nor Sandra said much at first. Then, Sandra made a tentative step by asking, "Are you mad at me?"

"Not at all. I mean it. I understand why you kept this secret from me. I do. I'm not mad."

"Then why are you acting so distant?"

"I'm just preoccupied."

"That's what I'm talking about. Right there. You're avoiding an answer by dismissing the whole thing, by being distant. Don't do that. That's the way we've always dealt with things. Avoid them until it blows up into a fight or a passionate night. Let's stop that. Tonight. You said no more secrets. I mean you've got to be wondering about me, right? So let's talk about it."

"I just want to be quiet and think." Throwing a charming smile, he added, "And we can still let this blow up into a passionate night later."

"No," Sandra said as she clutched Max's arm. "If everything is so fine, then I want to know why you're so far away. What are you thinking about?"

Max sighed and the sound reminded him of Drummond. He kept his eyes on the puddle, watching as the rain distorted the image thousands of times over. "For one," Max said, "we're about to commit a criminal act. That's not something I've had much experience with. For another, I only see Drummond. I don't know why I thought this, but I had assumed that was it. Not that Drummond was the only ghost but that he was the only one in the area — that ghosts were somehow few and far between. The idea that there are ghosts all over us — it's unsettling. I mean, are there any here now?"

Sandra glanced around the parking lot. "Do you see an old man leaning by that No Parking sign?"

"Nobody's there."

"Then there's one ghost."

Max shifted his weight and said, "That's just weird. I guess I'm also feeling strange about us. Not because of you or your ability or anything like that."

"Then what?"

"I'm sitting here and thinking about all the years I've known you, and I just wonder what our lives might've been like, how different, if I had known the real you. We've had such a screwy time lately, and maybe none of it had to actually happen. Maybe things could've been better. Maybe we never would have come down here and got all caught up with Hull." *Maybe you'd be quietly smiling over a rose every day.*

Sandra stroked Max's head. "You'll drive yourself crazy playing out all the What Ifs, and really, when you get to the end, none of that matters. This is the way it happened. This is the life we've got to live. Nothing you can say is going to change the fact that we're sitting here now listening to the rain, getting ready to break into an office," she said, curling the corner of her mouth which forced a warm smile from Max.

"No fair," he said.

"All's fair."

"Don't you do that hair flip thing."

"What? You mean this?" she said as she tossed her hair over one shoulder and leaned her head to the side, exposing her soft neck.

Max kissed her from the shoulder up to her ear. "Honey, I'm in love with you. Understand? You don't have to seduce me all over again."

"Maybe I want to."

"Then let's go home and forget about this place for tonight."

A moment passed in which Max thought she might agree. Then Sandra sat back, the glimmer in her eye turned icy, and she looked toward the office. "We've got to do this. You know —"

"I do, I do. It was just nice there for a minute to feel like a normal person again — one who doesn't have to worry about ghosts and curses and Hull."

"Is that her?"

A figure stepped outside, closed the door, and scurried toward a blue car holding a purse over her head. Because of the rain, Max found it difficult to tell if the figure was Dr. Connor — if not the doctor, she had to be an assistant. Once the blue car pulled away, there were no other cars in the parking lot.

"Guess this is it," he said.

Sandra kissed him. "I won't let anything happen to you."

They dashed across the street and toward the office. In just seconds, Max felt soaked through but he kept moving. And because of the cold and wet, Max did not hesitate when he reached the door but rather opened it with brazen abandon.

Inside the waiting room, they both shook off the rain. Sandra walked around the receptionist's desk, flicked on her flashlight, and started opening drawers. Max pointed his flashlight at her and said, "Forget about that stuff. It won't help us. If she has the book, it'll be back there, in her private ... lair."

"Lair?" Sandra said with a smile.

Max shrugged. "She's a witch, after all."

As they headed to the back room, Max listened for any sounds of people. He only heard the rain being blown against the building, their footsteps on the thin carpet, and his own nervous breathing. The air smelled different — partly a lemon-scented cleaner but mostly something stronger and stranger. It had a slight burned odor and a slight sweet aroma as if Dr. Connor had been lighting cinnamon sticks. Max tried not to think about the twisted spells that left such a smell in the air. He could not stop the chills rolling over his body.

When they reached Dr. Connor's private office, Max pointed to a bookshelf. "You look there. I'll check out the desk."

The desk was an exquisite, hand-crafted rolltop with fierce animal heads carved on the sides — snarling wolves, roaring bears, and gibbering hyenas. The shadows cast by the flashlight animated the carvings, and Max had to remind himself that it was just a desk. Dr. Connor was a witch and Drummond was a cursed ghost, but he didn't believe spells to bring wooden carvings to life were real. That seemed to be stretching reality in a way Max refused to accept.

In the desk, he found three books. Each looked very old and had been covered in thin, tanned hides. Sandra peeked over his shoulder and said, "You don't want to touch that."

"Why?" Max said as he picked one up. The covering felt smooth yet stuck on the book when rubbed.

"That's human skin."

With a gasp, he dropped it to the desk, the smooth feel of the cover still tingling his fingers like the remnants of an electric jolt. "A little warning next time would be appreciated."

"There's nothing on the bookshelf that fits the bill."

"What about these?" he asked, pointing to the rolltop.

"No. Human skin is used for very sacred texts. This is just a binding spell. From what you and Drummond said, this should be rather ordinary like a notebook or a journal or even a diary. Something easy to overlook."

Max glanced at the skin-covered books. Before his flashlight could play with the books shadows, he moved the beam to the floor. "Maybe she has a hiding space," he said. "A wall safe or a loose floorboard."

"I doubt it. Not if she's as powerful a witch as Drummond says. She has no need to hide a book, especially a minor binding book. If anything, she would have hidden those books you were looking at. No, if that book was here, it would have been in plain sight."

"Look here." Max pointed to a red, hardcover book with black lettering. "*Cruor Teneo*. That's on my office floor. Could this be it?"

"It means 'Blood Hold' and it's not what we want. That's more of an instruction book on various binding curses."

"Damn," Max said and slouched against the wall. "Without that book, I can't do anything for Drummond."

"Keep looking then."

"Why? You've made it clear that she doesn't have it here. It would be in plain sight and it's not. And for that matter, when I visited her the other night, she was trying to encourage me to find it. Why would she do that if she knew where it was?"

"If she has it, she obviously doesn't want you to know."

"Then why not dissuade me from even searching? I don't get it. I don't get a lot of what's going on. And you know what else? That book isn't here. So why should we keep looking?"

"Because what else can you do?"

"Leave here, for starters. If we were to get caught —"

The unmistakable sound of the front door opening echoed through the office. Without a word, Max and Sandra started scouring the room with their flashlights, each looking for a good hiding spot. Snapping his fingers at Sandra, Max indicated a door on the far wall. Light danced across the desk, the chairs, and the books, as they rushed to the door making as little noise as possible. With a gentle touch, Max turned the doorknob. The click it produced screamed in Max's ears.

"Kim?" Dr. Connor's voice called from the lobby. "Are you still here?"

"Go," Max whispered, following Sandra down a corridor that turned to the right. At the far end was an emergency door. The closer to the door, the faster they moved until Sandra pushed hard on the press bar, banging the door open. Max halted.

"What is it?" Sandra asked.

Max gazed up at her — his face pale, his eyes wide. "Stay here," he said and closed the door on her, leaving Sandra stuck in the rain.

As he hurried back up the corridor, he hoped he had not imagined the piece of paper. He had caught sight of it as they left the office. Amongst the books and shadows and odd-shaped statues, he had seen a paper with the Hull letterhead.

When he reached the door, he opened it with slow, careful motions. He peeked in after turning his flashlight off.

Nobody.

Flicking on the flashlight, he scanned the floor. As he moved into the office, the door behind him closed making a clear sound. Max heard approaching footsteps and Dr. Connor calling, "Hello?"

The flashlight's beam jittered across the room as the footsteps grew louder. "Whoever is in my office, you've made a big mistake."

Max edged backward toward the door, but still he

searched. Had he just imagined it? The next sound came from right behind the inner door — the witch chanting.

Spinning around, ready to race toward Sandra, Max saw the paper near the wall just to the left of the exit door. He grabbed it and another and dashed down the corridor. The chanting grew louder, and though he could never prove it, Max felt the air behind him pulling away — not a breeze or a wind but as if the air had a rope tied around it and was forced in a direction it did not wish to go.

When he burst outside, Sandra let out a yelp. He grabbed her hand and never stopped running. They went straight into the darkness of the night, never looking back, just pumping their legs until they both grew tired and cold in the rain.

Chapter 16

BY THE TIME THEY RETURNED TO THEIR CAR, drove home, and dried off, the clock read quarter-to-three and Max could not think clearly enough to deal with the papers he had stolen. Making sense of the word *stolen* in relation to himself was another matter entirely. Had he really become a thief? *It's just paper,* he thought. However, he dismissed such a weak response as the ramblings of his tired mind. Then he tried to dismiss all responses — clear his cluttered brain so that he might rest. Besides, unless he wanted to be haunted forever and pursued by Hull for-close-to-ever, this appeared to be his best option at the moment.

Sandra slumped on the couch with one paper in hand while Max looked at the other. With a yawn and a groan, Max leaned to read over Sandra's shoulder yet again.

SINGLE
VOGLER
SHULTZ
MIKSH
WINKLER
HORTON
BLUM
ACRE
SISTERS

"Names," Max said.

"Of who, though?"

"None of them stand out to me, but then, we haven't lived here that long. If the name were Reynolds, Hanes, or Hull, I'd know it, but these don't mean much of anything."

"Those marks can't be good."

Of the nine names, the last five had little dots in red ink. "Probably not," Max said. "Then again, maybe it's good to have the mark and bad not to — it could mean anything."

"It's not usually good to have a mark by your name." Sandra placed the paper into a tan file folder. "We should ask Drummond in the morning."

"You've done enough. I'll deal with Drummond."

"I'm not stopping now. I want to be a part of this."

"Really? I mean this is not a typical day for me. My work is rarely as nerve-wracking as this."

"I thought it was exciting."

"Most of my time is spent looking up things in books. Exciting is hardly the word for that."

With a look both amused and defiant, she said, "Honey, I'm involved now, and I'll see this thing through. We're in it together. Okay?"

"Then you should see this," he said, handing her the second paper.

"A letter?"

"Read it."

The paper was old and the penmanship hard to read. Sandra squinted and read aloud, "'My dearest Eve, I know you find yourself at a most difficult juncture. Two men vie for your heart and to your loving eyes, we must both seem worthy. Indeed, but a short fortnight ago I would have agreed with the sentiment, and though it would have left me heartbroken should you have chosen T—, no unbecoming scene would I have made. But the time has passed, and should this letter turn your adoring gaze from me forever, I feel it unforgivable should I let you embark upon marriage with T—- naïve to his true nature. He plans to leave, though you probably know as much, and he claims to seek out a greater church. What you do not know, however, is that he leaves not for love of another theology, not out of outrage toward our own failures, not for any noble or worthy cause, but from a demon's bargain. Hull (there, I have named him) has begun an exploration in the darkest of magics. His soul is most likely lost. Please, fairest Eve, I beg of you, do not lose your way to this power seeker. He will sacrifice your soul and laugh at your foolishness.'"

"There's no date," Max said, "but it sounds old. Maybe William Hull's grandfather. Certainly, the Hull family's been dealing with witches and magic for a long time."

"We have to be more careful than we thought," Sandra said, her eyes wide and frightened.

"We will be."

At six a.m. the telephone rang — a shrill sound that promised nothing good. Max and Sandra had fallen asleep on the couch, and both moved into consciousness with aches and groans. Max considered letting the answering machine take care of it, but Sandra shook her head. They both knew this would not be some early-morning drunk calling the wrong number. With a huff, Max reached across the couch to pick up the phone.

"Hello?"

The unmistakable voice of Mr. Modesto said, "Good morning, Mr. Porter. I'd like to have an update report."

"Okay," Max said, running his tongue over the film

covering his teeth. "What time?"

"I'm not available for a meeting with you at the moment. I'd like the report now."

"Now?"

"Is that a problem?"

"No," Max said, sitting taller and waving off Sandra's worried frown. "That'll be fine."

"Well, then, where are we?"

"Um ... I've done some preliminary research into the Old Salem area as you requested, and —"

"Preliminary? I expected you to have some viable properties lined up by now."

"I will soon," Max said, wondering how fast he could push something like this through when he had yet to do the most basic research. "Please understand that historic areas require a great amount of subtlety and patience; otherwise, you'll end up with people picketing outside your doorstep. There's always somebody who passionately wants to save every last old building that still stands."

"That is not your concern. We will handle such things, if they occur. You only need to come up with the best historical properties for our purchase."

"Historical? The papers you gave me stated you wanted high-valued locations. That's why I was looking near Old Salem. Now you specifically want historical buildings?"

"You know exactly what we want. Stop wasting my time. Do your job, or I'll see that our employer ends your association with us. Am I understood?"

"Yes, sir."

Modesto hung up. With her hand resting upon Max's shoulder, Sandra asked what happened. Max leaned back and let out a long breath. "I don't really know," he said before detailing the phone call. "Let's get cleaned up and go into the office. We need to talk with Drummond about that list. See if he knows who any of them are."

"We?" Sandra asked.

"You said it yourself — you're involved. Besides, I don't think I can do this on my own, and until Drummond is free, I am on my own."

As Sandra headed toward the bathroom, she looked over her shoulder and said, "You silly boy. You're never on your own."

An hour later, they arrived at the office. Taylor wasted time cleaning the already clean desk. Drummond walked behind him, knocking over papers and books, and chuckling as the young man bumbled about in an attempt to pick things up.

"Take the day off," Max said.

"You know I can't do that, sir," Taylor said as the book he placed on the desktop unbalanced itself and flipped to the floor. "Mr. Modesto told me —"

"I'll make your choice simple. If you stay here, I'm going to hit you."

"Sir?"

Max shoved Taylor. Sandra said, "Young man, you'd best get out of here. Mr. Porter's had a rough night."

Taylor took one clear look at Max and left the office at a brisk clip. Max tried not to laugh, but when Drummond burst into snorting hysterics hard enough to bring tears to his eyes had he been alive, Max let loose his own cackles. "That was fun," Drummond said.

"Unfortunately, the phone call I had this morning wasn't so fun," Max said, sobering as he explained the events of the previous night that concluded with Mr. Modesto's phone call.

Drummond took a seat and listened. His intense focus broke only the two times he glanced at Sandra. When Max had finished, Drummond drifted into the air and said, "This is all good news. Very good, as a matter of fact."

"But we didn't find the book."

"True. But we've found out enough so that Hull's people are getting worried. They came here this morning, as well."

Sandra perked up. "Really?"

"Modesto and Connor. She stood before me and spit out some vile words. Somebody ought to talk to her mother about that. I'm serious. If my mother caught me saying any of those nasty things, I wouldn't have been able to sit for over a week."

"Well, that lifts any doubt about Connor working for Hull. What did they do?" Max asked, scanning the office for any obvious signs of tampering.

"First, they threatened to put a new binding spell on me."

Sandra said, "I didn't think you could put one on top of the other. At least, not of the kind done to you before."

"That's right, and when I reminded them of that pesky little fact, they threatened to burn down the building which, when you consider that the symbols on the floor would become charred ash, would make it very difficult to release me from the binding. They said if you didn't come up with what they want, they'd destroy us all."

"Man, Drummond, I'm sorry."

"I don't really care about it. I mean, nice place and all, always was a good office, but they haven't got anything I want badly enough to give them what they want."

"They've got the book."

"Not if they're threatening to burn down this building. They acted coy, but come on, now, what else could they be after but the book? They know I'm after it. They fear what I might do if I were to gain my freedom. So, it's pretty clear that they don't have it either."

"Then why me?" Max asked. "I'm sick of this. Why go

to the expense of moving me down here, setting me up, giving me all this time-wasting research — I mean, they could've done all this on their own. It doesn't make any sense. I didn't have any connection to them. There's no logical reason to bring in a stranger. It only opens them up to outside scrutiny."

Sandra sat in Max's desk chair and folded her arms. "It seems to me that there are three key things going on here. First, there's the book, and I think we're all crystal clear on that one — we want it to set Drummond free, they want it to keep him in place, and nobody knows where it is. Then there's this old case regarding Stan Bowman. Obviously, this ties in with Drummond since it's the reason he's stuck here. So, perhaps they don't want us learning whatever you were getting close to finding out way back when."

"I'm right with you," Drummond said with a wink.

"Last is Max's employment. The Hull Corporation says it's buying up properties and wants an expert to research the area."

Scoffing, Max said, "I'm no expert. I'm good at research but hardly an expert."

"Well, they can't hire anybody too high profile. So, they hire you. Perhaps they know that the answers to the Bowman case or the book can be found in some land here. Perhaps this is all about attacking the same problem from different angles."

"Possibly," Drummond said. "In fact, that makes quite a bit of sense. After all, Hull is a large company. They can't go searching for this book or this land quietly — not under their own name. That would draw plenty of attention. But if they hired somebody ..."

Max nodded. "Somebody with no ties to the community. Somebody from the North that has no family or friends in the area. A couple with no children. A couple down on their luck that would dive in without too many questions. Okay, I'm sold. Now what?"

Drummond thought for a moment, circling the room in a wide arc. "I think Max should go hit the books again. See if you can find more about Hull."

"I've looked into the Hull family but there's not much. A Civil War reference but that's about it. The name doesn't really kick into use until Reynolds and Hanes become big."

"Amuse me. There's got to be something to find."

"They could just be paranoid. Perhaps they think there's something major hidden in the records, but there really isn't."

"Either way, you're the one to go find out," Drummond said and then pointed to Sandra. "You work at a bakery. What can you do?"

With a patronizing shake of her head, Sandra said, "You boys never talk, do you? Max, tell Drummond what I did right before the recession hit."

"You worked in a bar. What's that got to do with —"

"After that, honey. Use your brain."

Max slapped the desk. "I'm such an idiot."

"Yes, you are. I didn't want to step in your way, especially when we weren't really talking, but now I can help."

"Great," Drummond said with a scowl. "Now tell me what the heck you're talking about."

"Back in Michigan, I sold real estate."

"Wait a minute. You sold real estate?"

"Not commercial," Sandra said.

"That's not the point. Hull hired your husband as a researcher when they should've hired a real estate agent."

Max said, "Unless they wanted me to do research on more than just properties."

"Keep that in mind. This is getting weird in a way that

reminds me too much of the final days in the Bowman case. Everybody needs to be careful."

"Perhaps Sandra should look into recent real estate activities under the Hull name. Can you do that?"

Sandra nodded. "I still have some contacts."

"Good," Drummond said. "And I'll just float around here and play tricks on Taylor."

As Max and Sandra got up to leave, Max had another idea. "What about other ghosts?"

"What about them?"

Sandra said, "I don't see any others in here."

"That's 'cause I'm all alone. I don't have contact with other ghosts."

Max shook his head. "But you were able to make contact with that old guy, Sam. You got him to come here and see me. If you can do that, maybe you can find another ghost."

"And do what?"

"Maybe get a message through to the ghost community. Maybe somebody out there knows something."

"The ghost community? What the heck are you talking about? We're just dead. We don't have a community."

"How do you know? You've been stuck in here since you died. Maybe there's a thriving world of ghosts out there."

"Sandra, set your husband straight, please."

"I don't know," Sandra said. "I've seen lots of ghosts, and they always seem to be unaware of each other."

"That's right," Drummond said, clapping his hands.

"But then again, communities behave in all sorts of different ways. Max might be right."

Max smiled. "Besides, what else are you going to do all day. Picking on Taylor is going to get boring after awhile."

"You'd be surprised," Drummond said. "Okay, I'll try it,

but don't expect too much."

"Let's meet back here tonight for dinner. Hopefully, we'll all have good news to contribute."

"Aren't you the optimist?"

Max put his arm around Sandra and left the office. He didn't bother with a response other than to whistle a meandering tune. He wished he felt half as casual as he behaved, but a brave front helped him keep pressing forward. Having Sandra by his side helped more.

Chapter 17

THE MORNING DRAGGED ON FOR MAX as he rummaged through one useless book after another. As lunch approached, he closed the last book in his pile and resigned to the fact that no matter where he looked, he could not find anything helpful on the Hull family.

"I'll have to go talk with that old guy in Butner again," he said to the books. That sparked an idea. A second later he rushed to the nearest computer to search Butner and POWs. Only two books showed in the results but that was two more chances than he had before. Twenty minutes later, he had learned that bringing the POWs caused a bit of controversy and required Reynolds to smooth talk a lot of people.

"Yeah, but was good ol' Hull in the picture?"

Not surprisingly, Max found no references to Hull; however, the entire program smelled of the Hull Corporation. Next, he searched through the newspapers and found several articles about the POWs. One in particular announced the special transfer of seven Germans from Butner to Winston-Salem. All seven names were listed: Dietar Krause, Joseph Richter, Herbert Bauer, Günther Scholz, Stefan König, Fritz Keller, and Walter Huber.

Max jotted down the names. "It's a start," he said.

In the course of packing away his notes, he glanced at his scribblings from the first day — Moravians and Unitas Fratrum and the founding of Bethabara. The foundation for this little research construction project had proven quite unstable. "Wait just a moment," he whispered. Why would Modesto have started him out looking into all this old history if all he had wanted was the binding book?

Even as an idea formed in Max's head, he rushed toward the Special Collections room of the library. He spent a short time plugging in keyword searches until he found one promising entry. After handing in the request, he paced in front of the doorway as if expecting somebody to stop him at any moment. Then, before Max knew it, he sat in a private cubicle with the 1825 diary of Jeremiah Childress.

Bound in leather (throwing Max awful recollections of human skin bound books) and written in steep-angled, cursive lines, many of the entries proved to be mundane accounts of the Childress farm. "I know you've got something in there," Max said, turning a page. He learned that Childress was well-respected and that by 1828, he had been invited to become a member of the Elders Conference. Then Max read:

> *It is to my great dismay this twenty-first day of our Lord's year eighteen hundred twenty-nine that I must partake in a most unpleasant meeting of the Elders Conference. Our good man Thomas Christman, though perhaps I must restate his standing, has made it known his intentions to leave the warming fold of Unitas Fratrum. His soul has been poisoned by those who call themselves the Baptists. Indeed, Thomas claims he has stepped into the waters with their so-called holy men. I have known Thomas for many years, and though I cannot claim to be surprised by*

this development, I am, as I stated previously, dismayed. It is never a joyous occasion when we lose one of our own. Making this saddening situation worse is the indecent act dear Thomas has chosen to lay upon us. After receiving the Elders Conference's order to depart from Salem, Thomas shocked us all by refusing, such is his disdain for what he once held sacred. I am troubled by what has transpired since that moment of defiance. It was my fullest expectation that the Elders Conference would evict Mr. Christman from his home and send both he and his child away from Salem so as not to pollute the holiness and well-being of our citizens. That has not happened. In this action's stead, the Elders Conference voted not to evict as that would bring unwanted attention to our actions in the public forums. No, this honorable organization deemed it more appropriate to allow a soul-fouled man to retain ownership of his home until the Elders Conference could purchase the house from under its occupants. I spoke against this course and for my troubles discovered myself much alone.

Max skimmed through the next few days, discovering little of value. When he turned the page, however, he found more than he could have wished for.

Only one is willing to stand beside me and for that I thank the Lord for providing and His kindness and His grace. Tucker Hull is a young man in years but wise enough to despise this hypocrisy. We have shared numerous conversations and I believe he may understand our Lord's will better than any other I have ever conversed with. I consider him a friend. His comprehension of scripture far exceeds my limited fumbling and I do believe wholeheartedly that should he ask me I would willingly follow his leadership in any capacity he wishes. Truthfully spoken, I hold suspicions that he plans to remove himself, and those of us who support his ideas, for there are more than just myself, from the Unitas Fratrum and inaugurate a new Church, one unpolluted by the corruption of power, under his supervision.

Max stared at the name *Tucker Hull* for a full minute. He might have spent another five minutes sitting in shock, if not for the two women who walked by murmuring to the tune of their clicking heels. These sounds roused him, and with quiet, determined motions, Max copied down the diary entries. When he finished, he hurried back to the office.

Sandra and Drummond were waiting. Upon Max's entrance, Sandra gave him a quick hug and kiss. Drummond, however, burst into a rant that clearly had been rolling in his head for hours.

"Nothing," he said. "I tried everything I could, but they won't talk to me."

As Max took off his coat, he winked at Sandra and said, "You mean other ghosts?"

"What the hell do you think I've been doing all day? There's even one standing outside in front of the Y. I know he can see me. He glanced up here a few times, but he won't come in. He won't even shout something my way. And why? I never did anything to him. I don't even know the guy. Oh, I know the reason he'd give. Same reason I've heard ever since I got stuck here. Connor warned me — actually, she taunted me with this but it's ridiculous."

"You're losing me. What reason?"

"The binding. Pay attention. Connor said that I'd be

forever alone because no ghost would ever talk with me or be around me or anything if I'm bound. They fear they'll get caught in the binding, too. But this is important. I understand their worried and all, but if I saw some poor muck who had been cursed and I could help him, I'd be there right away. I can't believe none of these ghosts have any sympathy for me. It's downright immoral."

"I thought you didn't know about any other ghosts or a community or anything."

Drummond whisked over to the window, crossed his arms, and glared toward the street. "I may have misrepresented matters."

Max looked at Sandra. "How did it go for you?"

"Better," she said with a chuckle. "I found out that witchy-poo doesn't own her office and she doesn't lease it. She doesn't pay anything for it at all."

"Do I even need to bother guessing?"

"Oxsten and Son own it and they, according to your stock trace for Annabelle Bowman, are one of many dummy corporations. So, that's right, hon. Hull owns it. Owns most of the buildings on that block, actually."

"Hull lets Connor use the office for free but then he has access to a witch whenever he wants."

"There's more. This arrangement goes back well before Drummond was even born. Assuming all or most of the various companies named are dummies, and from what I can tell that is the case, then the Hulls have had a witch on retainer for over a hundred years."

Drummond said, "Two old family businesses. Figures."

"I also looked into this office building," Sandra said, and Drummond faced her. "It's also had a rather unorthodox history. Starts off fairly normal, changing hands a few times, but then the last owner disappears — I couldn't even find a death notice let alone a certificate. The building, however, keeps operating as if it had an owner. Nobody is named on any paperwork, yet no government action is taken. Then, out of nowhere, Hull assumes control. Their name is also missing from legal ownership, but they're the ones paying taxes, collecting rent —"

"Keeping this a cursed office for their own use," Max said.

"Pretty much."

"Good job, hon."

"Any time, dear."

"Enough," Drummond said. "You two have got to curb the mushy-mushy."

"The what?" Sandra said.

Before Drummond could take the bait, Max spoke up. "You guys won't believe what I found."

In a few minutes, Max explained how he found the diary and then, to Drummond's stunned silence, he read the entries. Sandra spoke first. "The Hull family goes all the way back to the seventeen hundreds."

"They go back to the foundation of this entire area. It's no wonder that by the time Bowman is working at R. J. Reynolds, the Hull family has money and power. They'd been at it for almost two centuries."

"You think this happened then — what this man wrote — that Tucker Hull defected from the Moravians to start his own church?"

"Read this," Max said, showing Eve's letter.

"You think this Hull is Tucker Hull?"

"Don't you?"

Drummond nodded. "So Tucker breaks away from the Moravians to start some evil magic religion."

Sandra nodded. "It's all interesting, but how does it help us, exactly?"

Max said, "I think it might help clear up a lot, but that's

all details. Right now, we've got to find that binding book."

"What about that list from Connor's office?"

"What list?" Drummond asked.

Max jumped to his feet. "I completely forgot. It's a list of names with some checked off. And I've got names of the Butner POWs. But I don't think they match. I'll start looking into them right away."

Drummond slid behind Max and read the list. "Those aren't people," he said.

"What are they, then?"

"Names of buildings in Old Salem."

"Old Salem," Max said. "There's no putting it off, now. I'll go right away."

"Slow down, there, kiddo. It's too late in the evening for that. You'll have to go in the morning."

Max checked the window — night. "Oh. Then let's get some sleep. Tomorrow, honey, see if you can find anything more to help us, and maybe check out the background on some of these buildings. I'll look into them directly in the morning. Drummond —"

"I'll just be floating around."

"Help out Sandra. Tell her whatever you know about this."

"Will do."

Max copied the building names on a yellow legal pad and gave it to Sandra. He surveyed the names once more before putting the paper in his pocket. "I'm wired, so I'm going back to the library 'til they close. I'll see what else I can learn. Don't wait up for me. First thing in the morning, I'll go to Old Salem. We'll meet here tomorrow night."

"Be careful," Sandra said.

"It's just Old Salem. I'm going to a public historical site. There'll be tons of people there, tourists, schools, and locals. What could possibly happen? Relax."

Chapter 18

THE NEXT MORNING, Max arrived at Old Salem. There were tourists, but not the thousands he had expected. In fact, if not for the people dressed in historically accurate garb, Old Salem could have been mistaken for any aging, quiet neighborhood. Of the one hundred buildings (so the lady at the Visitor's Center explained), ninety-seven were original, and for a modest price, he could tour all of them.

Before he even entered the town proper, Max knew this promised to be harder than he had expected. A detailed, covered bridge crossed the road below, linking the Visitor's Center to Old Salem's Main Street. Thick beams and struts crisscrossed to form a charming pattern. The strong, flavorful smell of hickory coated everything. Halfway across the bridge, Max stopped.

It could be here, he thought, *hidden in one of these beams.*

He walked back to the front of the bridge and searched with his eyes, looking at each minute detail. He glanced up and drooped with a sigh. Nailed over the entrance, Max saw an oval plate reading *1998* — too new to have an ancient book.

Main Street inclined a bit as Max walked across the old stone sidewalks. First stop was Vogler's Gun Shop established 1831. The building consisted of two small rooms. The front room had a wide-planked wood floor, a long work table, planks in the ceiling, several hand-crafted, period precise hunting rifles, and tools everywhere. A man with a white beard and small glasses smiled and said, "Welcome to the Gun Shop." He then went into his spiel, explaining all about the process of making weapons, the man who originally owned and operated the business, and how he would answer any questions Max had.

Max peeked into the back room. It was smaller and bore a rich, smoky odor. This was where the metalwork was done. A long wooden arm for pumping the bellows hung overhead. There were several anvils (one mounted on a tree stump), a trough of water, and plenty of ash that left the stone floor gritty.

As Max moved around the shop, he shifted his weight from one stone to the other, one wooden plank to the other, but too many of them creaked or moved — any one of them could be the cover to a hiding place.

Stepping back onto Main Street, he pulled out the paper and looked at the names once more. VOGLER did not have a little red dot next to it. Did that mean the witch had checked it out already and came up with nothing, or were the dotted ones the buildings already checked? He decided to ignore the dots since he couldn't be sure and instead headed up the street to the Shultz Shoe Shop from 1827.

This building was even smaller than the first — just one room no bigger than his office. A cast iron stove warmed the room from the back and a wooden table took most of the middle. To the right, sitting between two windows, were a man and a woman, each busy in the process of making shoes. "Hello," the shoemaker said, "and welcome to the Shultz Shoe Shop." Like the old man before, the shoemaker delivered his presentation from memory (though Max was impressed with how enthusiastic the people were after they gave their required talk). Like the other building, the floors here were made of wide planks and the walls were a solid wide plaster-like substance.

As Max pushed onward, a sensation he had become all too familiar with washed over his body — he was being followed. He tried to brush away the feeling, but the uneasiness refused to leave. He scanned the area — an old couple strolling hand in hand, a haggard father being dragged by an eager kid, a gaggle of ladies laughing and chatting. Nobody appeared to have the remotest interest in him. Nobody appeared out of place.

He entered a large house which the lady in the foyer explained was the Vogler House built in 1819 but presented as it was in 1840 (Max wondered if this was the same Vogler that also made guns but decided it didn't matter). On the left side were two connecting rooms — a parlor and dining room. On the right, Max found Mr. Vogler's workroom where he repaired watches and did other such detail work, and a kitchen. Each room was completely furnished with as many original pieces as the Historical Society could acquire.

In the dining room, a grandfather clock towered over him. It must have been near ten-feet tall. The lady in the room said that a man named Everhardt built and signed the clock, but Max could not recall the name from any of his research. It was such a beautiful piece (despite the crack running down the lower front) that even a novice like Max could appreciate it.

Upstairs, Max discovered four bedrooms — one of them a nursery with a crib and toys. Each bed, each writing desk, each planked floor held the promise of housing the book. However, the more he thought about it, the more he decided none of them could be the answer. These bits of furniture had been handled over the years by various members of the Historical Society. How could the book have remained undiscovered if it had been hidden in the crib or the writing tables?

The exit from the house was in the back, requiring Max to walk around in order to return to Main Street. As he turned the corner, he saw a figure dash into the house. It happened too fast to tell if the person was a man or woman or even if the incident was merely coincidence. However, the constant pressure forming on Max's shoulders and tightening his neck reminded him that sometimes being paranoid was warranted.

As he walked onward, he saw the town square on his right — a lovely, open area of grass and trees with four walkways forming an X. Pines circled the center and several benches lined the walkways. Though attractive and peaceful, Max registered little of the atmosphere around him. He only saw hundreds of places to hide a small item.

At the end of the block, on his left, stood a large building called Single Brothers. Max checked his list. The word SINGLE had no mark next to it.

Inside he found a three story home for single men to learn their trades in preparation for getting married. *My mother would love this,* he thought. To the left of the entrance was a wide room like a mini-church (the attendant informed him the room was called the Sall). A boxy white organ took up the back corner and plain, backless benches had been lined up in the center. Like many of the rooms Max had seen, this one contained what he thought to be an ornate heating stove along the wall. The stove had been painted a rich brown-red color, and like the others, this one could be an excellent place to hide something.

The options got worse as Max checked out the other end of the house. Here were numerous rooms, each devoted to a specific trade — joiners, potters, tailors, shoemakers. Downstairs, he found more — blue dyers, tin and pewter workers, and a carved door that led to a kitchen and small dining hall.

Enough, he thought. He was wasting his time with this and unnerving himself with every step that sounded like somebody following him. *But if I'm being followed, then perhaps I'm close to something worth keeping an eye on. After all, didn't Hull order Modesto to get me researching this area?*

Cold air blew across his forehead. Max looked up to find a small vent cooling the room for guests — most certainly not a historically accurate portrayal of colonial times. And, of course, another possible hiding place.

Max stormed out of the building and stomped his way back to his car. He hoped the others had fared better.

With a few hours left before he had to meet at the office, Max went back to the library. He didn't want to show up empty-handed, and he had the research itch attacking the back of his head.

It was those POWs. Too many questions. But now he had names, and names could be researched.

The amount of information regarding World War II would have been staggering had he not seen it before. Even in the subset of POWs (and just German ones no less), Max's searches turned up thousands of hits. Yet when he plugged in the specific names, things became more manageable.

Krause, Richter, and Bauer had little in their records to suggest anything noteworthy other than all three had visited the States prior to the war. Schulz and König were strong men with families and neither had any contact with the U.S. previously. Fritz Keller was the most educated of the lot and had authored several articles in German newspapers before being called to duty. And Walter Huber proved to be the criminal of the bunch. In less than six months upon returning to Germany, he ended up in prison for armed assault. Nothing singled any of these men out.

"Not that I even know what I'm looking for," Max said to the computer screen.

One odd piece of information did perk up, however. Max found an artist's website that included dramatic collages made from World War II paperwork. The papers were chosen to match a theme — a picture of a gaunt Jewish prisoner had been made from Auschwitz population lists; a tribute to the fallen soldiers of D-Day came from copies of Eisenhower's famous orders; and there was even a German POW made from transfer papers.

Max spent close to an hour magnifying each small section of the collage, looking for any of the names, and to his surprise, he came upon the name Butner. Two sheets from about a week apart. The first showed the release orders for seven POWs to be sent to RJR. The second showed a return order, and though it was difficult to read, Max thought the sheet only showed six POWs returning.

"We got nothing," Drummond said before Max could kiss his wife or even sit at his desk.

"Speak for yourself," Sandra said.

"Doll, you were just saying that you didn't turn up anything else. Now that Max is back here, you going to make up some flimflam so you look good for your lover?"

"I swear, you act like you were a teenager when you died."

Max blotted out their noise as long as he could manage. When he couldn't take anymore, he raised his voice and said, "Do you have something or don't you?"

"Honey, relax."

"See," Drummond said, "You're making Max all tense."

"Be quiet. Now, Max, I found out that the Old Salem area is still active. It's not just public, historical buildings. Many of them are privately owned residences. The owners have a strict set of rules they have to follow to preserve their buildings, but they do live there."

Max nodded. "The lady I got my ticket from mentioned something about people still living there. It just makes matters worse. I went into several of the buildings and walked the streets. That book could be anywhere, and now you're saying it could be in a private residence."

"You're not letting me finish."

"Sorry. Go ahead."

"I found out that two of the buildings have been very quietly put on the market."

Max leaned forward. "How much are they going for?"

"Nobody'll tell me, but I wouldn't doubt for a second that Hull could buy them if he wanted to."

"I think he just might."

Drummond brushed by Max, Max's arm feeling as if it had been dashed with icy water, and said, "Looks like we have a bit of a pickle."

"What now?" Sandra said.

"Easy there, I'm just pointing out the fact that if you intend to find this book before Hull, you've got to do it before he buys those homes. Unless you can purchase them."

Sandra said, "It might not even be in those homes."

"That's right," Max said. "All of the building names on the list are buildings open to the public."

"But if it is in one of these private houses, you lose. If it isn't, Hull has a central location from where he can conduct all the searches he wants. Every night, he can check out each one of those old buildings until, voila, he finds his little treasure."

"Then we've got trouble. I was told there's a good chance Hull will make an offer in the next day or two. Well, actually it's that company Oxsten and Son, but of course, that's Hull."

Max glanced out the window. A chubby fellow with a thick mustache hustled up the sidewalk, a blue coffee mug in his hand. Across the street, a woman with her baby in a stroller walked by the YMCA. Normal life.

"I might be able to stall Hull for an extra day," Max said. "After all, I'm supposed to be researching this kind of thing for him anyway. Perhaps if we give him some misinformation, he'll waste a day or two checking it out."

"Ah," Drummond said with a lascivious smile, "we're finally getting into a little deception here. I like it."

Sandra said, "We still have the problem of the book itself. You said it could be anywhere in there."

"Well, true," said Max. Then he paused. An idea popped in his mind, one he knew would work, but he worried about suggesting it. The idea of using his wife, even if in a harmless manner, did not sit well. He could hear Drummond's reply in his head — *Better to use the wife than end up like me*. "I have a thought," he finally said.

"Congratulations," Drummond said.

"Let me meet with Modesto to try to stall Hull. Then, tomorrow night, Sandra and I could go to Old Salem together and you could —" He looked long at his wife. "— well, I'm sure there's a lot of ghosts around there."

Drummond perked up. "Hey, that's great. You could just ask the locals where this book is. Some of them may have even been there when it was hidden in the first place."

Sandra shook her head. "This is not a good idea."

"I don't think we have a better alternative," Max said as he sat on the desk's edge.

"I know, but I haven't told you everything about ghosts. See, when they're not bound like cheerful here, they're a lot different."

"How?"

"More capable."

Drummond pouted. "Hey. I'm plenty capable."

"What do you mean?" Max asked.

Sandra stared right into Max's eyes. "I mean they might not be so friendly, so willing to help. And they might be able to hurt us."

Chapter 19

WHEN MODESTO ARRIVED AT CITIES RESTAURANT for their regular meeting, he looked haggard — still immaculate to most eyes, but Max knew better. His hair perfect but for a few strands, his clothes sleek but for a subtle wrinkle, Modesto moved toward the table with an urgency that lacked grace. With his face crinkled in worry, he fumbled a greeting. Max tried to put these observations out of his mind. He had one job to do in this meeting — buy some time.

As Modesto slipped into his seat, he said, "What's been your progress in Old Salem?"

"Old Salem?" Max said, tinting his expression with as much innocence as he thought Modesto would swallow.

Modesto frowned. "You do recall who is paying your bills?"

"There's no need to be hostile."

"It seems your extra-curricular activities are clouding your judgment. So, let me ask this way: what exactly do you have for me today?"

"Why did you hire me?"

Modesto shook his head. "Mr. Porter, if you have failed in your duties, then please stop wasting my time and admit you have nothing to offer me. If you have information, then let me have it. I am extremely tired and our employer has not been pleased with you so far."

"I've done an excellent job. You asked for research on the Moravians, and I provided. You wanted research on various land deals, and I provided. I'm good at what I do."

"Then you have your answer, don't you? That is why you were hired."

"Why is he dissatisfied, then?" Max watched Modesto's face contort as the man strived for an answer that would not betray anything.

"I do not claim to understand the ranking system of our employer," Modesto finally said. "I am merely reporting his concerns to you."

Max said nothing for a moment, enjoying every second of Modesto's squirming. Even in the way they looked at each other through sideways glances and indirect observations, both men were dancing around the facts. "In that case," Max said, "let our employer know that you've informed me of his displeasure. If he desires to fire me —"

"He does not."

"I'm confused. I thought you said he felt my work was unsatisfactory."

"Just focus on your report."

"No, sir. Not when the quality of my work has been called into question."

Modesto glanced upward as if asking for strength. *Or perhaps,* Max thought, *he's looking at what liquor they have on the wall.*

"I assure you, I have found your work superior to most. I give you my word I shall state my satisfaction in my next report. Beyond that, there is little for us to discuss on the matter because I cannot speak for our employer on the subject. Is that enough for you?"

"A little appreciation is all I ask. Thank you, sir."

"What do you have for me?"

"There's one building in Old Salem up for sale."

"Just one?" Modesto asked, and Max saw in his eyes he not only knew that there were two, but he knew Max had lied.

"You'll find the details and my assessment in the folder," Max said, pushing a blue folder across the table. "Little company called Oxsten and Son is in position to take it. I can't find too much about them, but I will eventually. There might be more homes available soon, though. Including one near the Vogler house." This part was an entire fabrication, but Modesto's eager ears perked up, and Max knew he had bought a few hours while Modesto wasted time trying to find out anything about the fictitious house.

"Near the Vogler house."

"Yes, not on the market yet, but my wife has a friend in real estate who mentioned it in passing, so I'm doing the same. I hope you don't mind me using her for a little information. She doesn't know that I'm giving it to you, so don't worry about that."

"No problem."

"Would you like me to keep looking?"

Modesto stuffed the folder in his briefcase and said, "Yes, that would be fine. I'll review your work and we'll decide then what to do."

"I did uncover some interesting points concerning the area. Just a few things that might be of use to our employer."

"Oh?"

"For example, the Moravians put in the first waterworks system right here in Old Salem. Pipes and plumbing and such to bring running water into the homes."

"Mr. Porter, we are well aware of the basic knowledge available from an Old Salem tour."

"You're missing the point."

"And this would be?"

"Obviously I don't know anything specific about our employer but it seems clear that he is interested in antiquities of all kinds. Why else the search for old history and old land? I figured if he could acquire some of these ancient pieces, they would be worth a lot of money."

"I see."

"Another little tidbit I found was that during World War II, the Reynolds family used German POWs to help make cigarettes and such."

"Also a widely-known fact," Modesto said in a way that sounded more like a threat than a statement.

"My mistake. I just thought there might be old bits of memorabilia and such from the Germans, just something of value for the antiquities trade."

Modesto stood, regaining his composure so fast that Max thought he had pushed too far. With a slight bow of the head, Modesto said, "I don't think you're a very smart man."

"Gee, thanks."

"You don't lie very well and the choices you've made seem to be less than logical. I can't imagine how you manage to survive the rigors of life."

"Perhaps I'm not much of a liar, but I don't need to be one for this kind of work. All I need is for the person I'm talking with to be a liar as well."

"Excuse me?"

For the first time since Modesto had arrived, Max looked straight at him. "When you lie, you make it difficult to expose another's lies and near impossible to reveal the truth. It's a case of mutually assured destruction."

"Good day, Mr. Porter," Modesto said and left the restaurant.

Max waited until his food arrived. As he ate, he kept

thinking about the little taunts and jabs he had used against Modesto. He had hoped to get Modesto riled enough to slip up with some information regarding Old Salem. Instead, he got little to help save for one thing — his own words. Max had mentioned the possibility of World War II memorabilia still in existence in the area. Perhaps he was right. Perhaps he should take a visit to Annabelle Bowman.

"What do you want?" Annabelle asked from behind her screen door. Her stern brow and hard glare invited little opening for reconciliation — not that he had expected a warm welcome.

"Please, Ms. Bowman, just a few moments of your time."

"I'm done talking with you."

"It's important."

"Go away. I'll call the police."

"I doubt the Hull family would be too keen on the police poking around why I'm here."

That got her. She glanced behind and when she looked back, her troubled eyes undercut her icy face. "If I let you in," she said a bit softer, "they'll hurt ... I ... I don't want this. Please, just go."

"I don't want you to get hurt. I just need to see a few things of Stan's — stuff he kept during the war, during his time at Reynolds, that kind of thing."

With a bit of the cold returning, she said, "I know what you want, but you can forget all about it. I told them the same thing. I destroyed it all. Hull wanted it gone and it's gone. So, let an old woman alone."

"The longer we argue out here, the more likely it is that somebody is going to see us."

"Shit," she said under her breath, opened the door, and

rushed Max inside. "Now, look, I'll give you five minutes and then I want you out of here. Do you understand? You stick around any longer and I will call the police and I'll tell them you tried to rape me or murder me or something, but I assure you whatever I come up with will be ugly enough to divert all attention from Hull and me."

"Fair enough," Max said, hoping just to keep the lady talking. His eyes searched the room he sat in the last time he had visited — something had to be here, something from Stan. "I'm just trying to help out a friend. He was involved with Stan back during the whole affair and, well, I just need to clear up a few details. That's all. I promise."

"And what friend is that?"

"Considering how worried you are, it's best you don't know," he said, more confident about his skills than the last time he interviewed this woman but still knowing Drummond could do far better.

"Why can't you all just let that be buried?"

"I wish I could," Max said, as he read book titles, noted old pictures, and spied a dying fern in the corner. Nothing useful. *This is stupid,* he thought. *I'm fishing and I don't even know how to hold the rod.* Just before he apologized his way outside, he processed the words she said only a moment earlier — that she knew what he had come for and something about others coming for it as well. He pictured how Drummond would handle the matter, wiped away all the rudeness, and attempted a suave smile. "Listen, you're a nice lady and I don't want to cause you any more trouble than I have to."

"Then get out of here and leave me alone."

"I can't leave until you give me what I'm here for."

"I don't have it. I never did. Everybody thinks Hull and I were so close, but I'm telling you I never saw any book. After Stan had his troubles and I cleaned out his old footlocker, I did find ... but none of it matters anymore. So let it all rest."

"Hull came to you for a book of Stan's?"

Wiping her hands on her legs, she nodded. "After Stan died. Mr. Hull visited me several times."

"Is that when he bought you stock in RJR?"

"He felt terrible about everything that had happened to Stan and wanted to help me out. At least, that was what he said to me. But he really wanted Stan's book."

"What's in the book?" Max asked and the second the words left his lips, he knew had made a mistake.

Annabelle's posture stiffened and she tapped her watch. "Time for you to go. And I mean it this time. I will call the police. So, please, go."

"But —"

"And don't ever come back again. You are no longer welcome in my home."

Max sipped a mug of hot chocolate at the kitchen table. Sandra stirred her tea from the opposite side. The little wall clock ticked sharp and clear in the otherwise silent room.

At length, Sandra said, "I'm a little scared."

"Me too."

"I just wish we could pack up and leave."

Max set his mug on the table. "You wouldn't believe how many times I've had that thought. You know what, though? These things never leave you. You can't outrun them. Isn't that why we left Michigan — just running away from our problems? But look where we are now."

"This is different."

"I don't think so anymore. When I saw Annabelle Bowman today, I saw an old lady with a lot of fear and regret. Whether she knows about all the witchcraft and Hull and ghosts, who knows? But it doesn't matter. None of that changes anything. No matter how much she pretends the past is over, she can't outrun this. And in the end, because she won't deal with it, she's still just an old lady with a lot of fear and regret."

"Is that supposed to comfort me?" Sandra asked. They both shared a quiet smile and held hands across the table.

Max leaned his head back and said, "Did I ever tell you about Archie Lee?"

"I don't think so."

"He was a guy I knew back in college. I think he was Korean. Well, Asian, anyway. Isn't that horrible? I should know something like that."

Sandra shook his hand. "You got a point to all this?"

"Just that, I remember sitting with him in this house — it was at a party at somebody's house, and he was telling me all about his life. I must've said something to get him going or maybe he was just so drunk he'd have told anybody but he told me about how he had moved around a lot since he was seven years old. I forget how much but it was as if every other year he had to up and move to a new state or a new country or whatever. And he said that, at the time, he learned to love it because he got to try out new personalities with each new place. I remember him telling me that he knew he was a bit of a nerd, and when he would move, nobody knew anything about him. He could pretend to have been the coolest, most popular kid from his old school. He would wear the cool clothes, get the right haircut, the right book bag, whatever it took. Who could say otherwise?

"But then he got real silent. I thought it was the beer finally getting him down but he grew very serious and shook his head slowly. He said that it never worked. That no matter what he tried, eventually, the new kids would figure out that he was just a nerd."

"You think we're just nerds?" Sandra said.

"The reason Archie Lee was still a nerd was because he had focused only on changing the outside. It didn't matter how many times he moved. Nothing was going to change for him because he kept paying attention to the wrong things."

"Still waiting for the comforting thoughts in all this."

Max drank some more of his hot chocolate. "If we were to pack up and leave, run off to some other job in some other state, we'd end up stuck in it just like this time."

"Nothing is like this time."

"Okay, well, maybe not the exact same thing, but the point is we'd still be the same people making the same choices we always make. But if we stay, if we fight our way through all this, then maybe we can improve ourselves enough to make things different. I don't know, make things better. Besides, aren't you the one who told me we had to push through?"

Sandra said nothing for a few minutes, then she looked upon Max and said, "You know something? I love you."

Part of Max wanted to talk this out further, but he tried to listen to his own words. The old way was talk and talk and talk until every angle and emotion had been explored. In the end, they would make love, but the next morning, nothing much would change. This time, Max decided, would be different. This time, he would take her love and hold onto it, forget about analyzing it to death, and instead, draw on its strength. After all, they were about to go ghost hunting in Old Salem. He needed all the strength he could get.

Chapter 20

THEY PARKED ON SALT STREET, a quiet area dominated by one ancient tree and a wall of younger trees, and in full view of the backyards of the houses lining Main Street. Light drizzle fell, and the midnight moon glossed the wet pavement with a dim, quarter-crescent glow. The sound of water drips hitting fallen leaves peppered the air. Though people lived here, nobody appeared to be up at two in the morning.

"See anything?" Max whispered.

Sandra peered around. "There's a dog sniffing that tree."

"You see dead animals, too?"

"No. There's a real dog sniffing that tree."

Max followed Sandra's eyes and saw a small, black Dachshund puttering around a maple tree. Stifling a nervous giggle, Max said, "Let's just get to this."

Sandra pecked his cheek and headed up the street. "Honey, relax. We're just talking to some ghosts."

"There's a sentence I never thought I'd hear."

"I mean it. You've got nothing to fear."

"You're the one who said they can get all angry and hurt us when they're not bound."

"But you're with me. I won't let them harm you."

"You know some special handshake or something?"

"Let's just get this done," she said and turned onto West

Street at a fast clip.

Max hurried to catch up. "Where to first?" he asked.

She gestured toward the town square. "That seems like the best place to start. I'll be able to see a lot of the area from the center."

Together they walked toward the grassy square, a truck passing on a distant street the only sound not of their making. Max listened to their breathing, their footsteps, their nervousness. *More than just fear,* he thought. If a person's imagination could have accidentally altered reality, he knew he would be bringing terrible creatures upon them. The idea of abandoning this pursuit, of rushing back to their car's safety and slipping home, seduced him for a fleeting moment. Then they arrived at the center, ringed by tall evergreens scenting the air with their wet fragrance.

"Okay, ready?" Sandra asked. Max could only nod. Sandra took a cleansing breath and turned in a slow circle. Her eyes darted about. She squinted at one spot, glossed over another, until she returned to the position where she had started. Another breath, another slow circular turn, another return to the start.

Max started to speak but Sandra snapped her head to the side. "What is it?" he asked, peering over her shoulder toward the Salem Academy. "What do you see?"

"I don't know," she said. "Not a ghost. At least, not like the ones I've always seen. This was more like a wisp of smoke, like black smoke that moved of its own will. But I didn't see anything solid."

"This place is hundreds of years old. Most of these buildings are original. It should be teeming with ghosts. Shouldn't it?"

"What are you talking about?" Sandra said, raising her voice enough to sound violent in the still night air. "What do you know about it? You've seen one ghost and you think you understand it? I've been dealing with this my whole life, and I've been doing it on my own — no formal training, no mentor, nothing. So forgive me if I can't make it all work just the way you want it on cue."

Max stepped back. "I didn't mean it that way. I don't feel comfortable here. I want this to be over. That's all." But that wasn't all. He didn't want to tell her that he had caught sight of the black wisp, too, and to him it was not a shadowy spirit at all, but rather a shadow — they were being watched.

"There," Sandra said and pointed in the opposite direction of the shadow.

"What do you see?"

"I don't know yet. Something, though. A faint glimmer of something," she said and headed across the slippery grass.

Max followed, glancing over his shoulder several times but never catching even a glimpse of the shadow he had seen before. Perhaps it was just an overactive imagination playing on his nerves. The idea made sense, but Max just couldn't believe it.

Sandra crossed the street and stepped onto the brick laid sidewalk. Old trees pushed up the bricks with their roots, making the path a series of miniature mountains and valleys. She knelt down and smiled into empty space. "Hello," she said. Max squatted behind her but he saw nothing. "You're very pretty ... I can't hear you too well," she said. Then she jumped to her feet. "Wait! Come back!" Wiping the damp hair out of her face, she turned to Max. "She disappeared. Damn. I don't think she knew, you know? That she was dead? I must've scared her pretty bad."

"Don't be ridiculous. I'm sure she runs from ghost-seeing people all the time."

Sandra responded with just a hint of a smile — enough

to ease them both a little. "This is going to be tricky," she said. "Don't worry, though, we'll get one of them to help us."

Together they stood on the sidewalk, each silent, each searching the empty grounds. Max checked every window, every doorway, every nook he thought might harbor an enemy.

An enemy? The idea that he now had faceless enemies to contend with, had been contending with for some time, eroded any illusion of security he still horded. *Come on, ghosts,* he thought. *Show yourselves already.*

Another five minutes passed before Sandra said, "On the corner." She waved and approached like a tourist seeking a little friendly information — not too far from the truth, in fact. "Excuse me," she said, "I'm looking for a book that was placed around here awhile back ... a book ... no, no, a book." To Max, she said, "I think we're supposed to follow."

"Then let's follow."

Max kept a few steps back from Sandra so as not to crowd her or her invisible companion — plus, it afforded him a better distance to react from in case somebody moved against them. Not that he had an inkling what to do should anything happen, but some chance was better than none at all. Watching the sway of his wife's hips sent a jolt through his body — he would rather be at home in bed with her than traipsing in the drizzle, but then he'd rather never have heard of Hull or any of this in the first place.

"This way," Sandra said, pointing to the long building Max had toured during daylight — Single Brothers House.

"How do we get in?" Max asked as he jiggled the locked door handle.

"I think," Sandra said and they heard a click from behind the door. "Looks like our ghost is being helpful."

"Let's just keep on his good side."

Sandra frowned. "How did you know that?"

"I assume an angry ghost would not be a good idea."

"No, you said *his*. You said, 'Let's just keep on *his* good side.' How did you know the ghost was male?"

Had it been broad daylight, had they not been talking about ghosts of long dead settlers, he might have had a flippant or sarcastic reply. Instead, under the thin moonlight and steady drizzle, his chest grew heavy. "I don't know," he whispered, afraid to think the question through. "Just a guess." Without waiting for a response, he tried the door handle again and this time it opened with ease.

They stepped into the wide foyer, the hollow sound of their footsteps on old wood echoed throughout the empty building. A musty odor tickled Max's nose, thicker than when he had visited before, and though rather open in design, Max felt the walls tightening around him in the darkness. He fumbled for his flashlight, and when he flicked it on, the narrow, pale beam made the claustrophobic sensation worse as if only the illuminated sections of the building existed.

Sandra drew a quick breath. "Wow," she said.

"Ghosts?"

"Just two others, but they're impressive looking. Their light is so bright."

Max moved the flashlight around but saw only an empty foyer. "Can you see our fellow?"

"It's hard," she said, squinting in the dark.

"Call him. Maybe he can still hear you."

"Shh. Please, let me do this."

Max waited, wondering what the ghosts were doing, where they stood. Did they see him? Did they feel his presence? Perhaps that's why he felt so closed in — perhaps he felt them surrounding him.

Sandra turned right and crept down the trade hall. The joiner's room on the right looked menacing in the flashlight beam — wooden skeletons of unfinished furniture surrounded by tortuous tools of assorted sizes. They proceeded further down the hall. The potter's room on the left with its foot-powered spinning wheel turned into a macabre lair where strange experiments of creation occurred under their nighttime gaze. Then, to Max's dismay, the ghost led them downstairs to the darker, colder basement floor.

Max struggled to recall the pleasant daytime feel of this building but even the scuffling of their feet against the stone floor transformed into a hideous monster lurking just beyond the flashlight beam. He followed Sandra and the ghost down the hall until they stopped at a door on the left. A placard on a podium explained that this room had once been used for training but later came to be a storage room. Sandra stepped over the rope barring the entrance and pointed to a dusty pile of junk filling up the corner.

"I think it's in here," she said and started sifting through the pile.

Max entered the room to help. Broken pottery and old wood scraps lay around, haphazardly discarded in the room. A broom, a mop, bits of paper, and other leftovers filled in the numerous nooks of the small room. When Max pulled out a large, metal hook, Sandra said, "Crap."

"What?"

To the empty space, she said, "Book. I said, 'Book.' With a *B*. Damn."

Letting the hook clatter to the ground, Max said, "Great."

"Don't go," she said, stepping toward the outer-wall. Then her shoulders drooped. "He's gone."

"I'm sorry, honey, this was just a bad idea. These ghosts

aren't going to help us."

"That's only the second one. We've got to give it more time. It's not easy. Not all ghosts are as connected with the world like Drummond. Some of them are barely here at all. It's like trying to get directions during a snowstorm in Siberia and you don't speak Russian. Get it?"

"I know. I'm not blaming you. But, really, this could go on all night with no luck."

"Or we might hit it big."

Max heard wood creaking from above. "Shh," he snapped and turned out the flashlight. With slow, quiet movements, he edged toward Sandra. He stepped into the corner of something sharp, pain bursting at his hip, and grunted as he wrangled back the urge to yell. He felt around — the podium with the placard. Inching a few steps at a time, he worked around the podium and reached Sandra, put his mouth to her ear and whispered, "I think somebody's been following us since we got here."

"How do we get out?" she asked, her voice steady despite her rigid body.

"To the left and upstairs there's a door. It leads out back to the gardens. When we go, I'll turn the flashlight on and keep it pointed straight at the ground. At the stairs, I'll turn it off and the rest we have to do in the dark. Move quick but not so fast that you'll get hurt. And ... I don't know. That's the best I can come up with."

"It's plenty good."

"I love you, you know."

"Right back at you," she said, turned her face and pressed her lips against Max with such force that his chest swelled with an overwhelming sensation — love and dread swirling like two wrestlers forever clenched together.

When she pulled back, she exhaled slow and deliberate. "Okay. I'm ready."

"Okay," he said, "I'm turning on the flashlight. Get ready to move. Here we go."

Max pushed the flashlight's button, and it blazed light onto the floor. He saw the podium and the various piles of wood and boxes, and in the doorway, he saw the figure of a man lunging toward him.

Chapter 21

TOGETHER, MAX AND SANDRA let out a startled cry. The man leapt atop Max and the flashlight banged to the floor, shutting off, leaving them in darkness. Max shoved hard but could not budge his attacker. Two strong hands gripped his throat, pushing his head back and slicing his ear against the corner of some plywood. Again, Max attempted to push off the man but the struggle for air weakened him.

"Max? Max?" Sandra called as she fumbled in the dark. He wanted to reach out to her, to hold her hand, and the thought flashed in his mind that, at least, it wasn't her throat being strangled at the moment. He pictured this man straddling her, choking her, and hoped she had the sense to run now while she could get away.

The image in his mind brought to the forefront that he should have done what any sensible woman would have attempted from the beginning. Mustering the last of his strength, Max garbled out a yell and rammed his knee upward into the man's groin. His knee hit something hard and he heard a crack. The man grunted a cry and rolled to the side, curled in a fetal position and whimpering.

Max wheezed and gasped as he crawled forward, one hand massaging his throat, the other seeking the flashlight. The fight had sent ages of dust into the air, drying out Max's mouth with its dead taste. Blood dribbled from his ear. He felt a hand grab his wrist, but before he could utter a painful yelp, he heard the welcome voice of his love.

"It's me, it's me," she said. "I can't find the flashlight."

He pulled her hand towards his chest and breathed in her hair. Together, they stumbled to their feet and groped a path into the hall.

"This way," Max said, every syllable searing his throat. He turned left and moved as fast as he dared in the darkness. When he reached a wide door, slants carved into the wood, he searched for a handle or knob.

The door wouldn't open. *Calm down,* he scolded himself. *Don't panic.* "I think it's locked," he said.

"Be sure," Sandra yelled.

"We're wasting time. That guy's not going to be down for long. He was wearing a cup, for crying out loud. A fucking cup. What kind of person wears a cup?"

"A professional, honey."

"That's what I'm saying. Now, let's go back the way we came. I can get us out of here."

"But the door."

"Sandra, trust me."

He heard the rustling of her clothing as she nodded. Then he heard something that shot adrenaline through his body — silence. Why didn't he hear the groans of their enemy?

"Sandra," he whispered. Her hands fidgeted about his arm until they found his right hand again where they affixed firm. Without another word, he led her back down the hall, his left hand trailing the rough wall.

He heard the grunt a second before he felt the man's fist strike his lower back. Max arched as the man grabbed his head and tossed him into the wall. His left arm blocked much of the impact, but still he saw little blue flashes in the darkness.

He heard Sandra scream. He heard the man yell. He heard a body smack into something hard and drop. As he forced himself to stand (he only just noticed he had fallen to the floor), Max felt hands grab hold of his arm. He yanked back, flailing in the dark.

"It's okay. It's me," Sandra said.

"Where's —"

"I don't know. He grabbed me and I bit his hand. Then I swung my fist and hit him — I think in the head but I'm not sure. I can't see anything. Can you walk?"

"I'm okay," Max said, wrapping his arm around her shoulder and using her as a crutch. His head blazed, and he wanted to vomit but managed to keep setting one foot in front of the other.

They reached the stairs and clambered up to the main floor. Light from the streets pierced the darkness in sharp slivers — enough to move fast. Max took three deep breaths, let go of Sandra, and focused on walking in a straight line. Each step sent stabs up his side but he pushed on. Knowing the danger just one floor below motivated him plenty.

Sandra darted ahead, reached the backdoor and rattled the handle until it opened. He could see her triumphant smile. "I got it," she said.

She put her arm around his waist for support, and together they stepped into the backyard, light rain dancing on their faces and filling the chill night air with its fresh smell. They hurried along the path leading to the garden and the fenced-in crops. Max expected to hear the man slam open the door and chase after them but nothing came. Not yet. Sandra slipped on the wet ground, causing Max to stumble as well, but they managed to stay standing and rushed to the garden's end.

"Can you climb over?" Sandra asked.

The fence was made of wood and only chest high, but Max knew the climb would hurt. The idea of going back and around the fence did not sit well, though, so he nodded. Wincing and grunting, and with the aid of Sandra, he managed the small feat.

"The car's this way," Sandra said, heading left.

"No," Max said. "They might be waiting for us."

"They? There's more than one?"

"I don't know, but we're not risking it. Let's go around, take the long way, and we'll circle back. If there's only one or a whole gang it won't matter. Either they'll have left by that time or we'll be able to see them as we approach. We'll know then and figure it out from there."

"Okay," she said, scanning the area. "We're on Old Salem Road."

"Follow it to the right. I think it curves a few blocks up and connects with Main Street."

As they walked along the glistening street, several cars shot by. Max felt too unsteady for this street. He kept seeing himself weave into the path of an oncoming car. With a nod, he led Sandra back onto Salt Street, heading away from their car and paralleling Old Salem Road.

He checked over his shoulder for any pursuit. Just empty street. White streetlamps dotted the right side of the road, one with a white street sign — the paint chipping off. The left side had a brick sidewalk and homes. The cracked pavement pooled water. A weird sensation formed in Max's chest, worked upward until it reached his face, and emerged with a fit of giggles.

"What are you laughing at?" Sandra asked, smiling at his infectious sound.

Max tried to suppress the noise, clamping his mouth down, but it only served to strengthen the laughter until it burst from his nose. He shook his head as he laughed, wiped his tearing eyes, and said, "I'm just thinking about that guy. He's all acting tough and then Wham! You nailed him." The laughter erupted again.

Sandra joined in. "I wish it hadn't been so dark. Can you picture his face? Duh!" she said and crossed her eyes. Max laughed so hard he stopped making sound and clutched his side in pain yet unable to stop smiling. After a few more feet, they had to sit on the wooden steps of a house until all their tension had been released. With a cleansing breath, Max said, "Oh my. We shouldn't laugh. When we get back we should call the police or somebody. That guy might've gotten hurt."

"So what? You really care what happens to him? He tried to kill you."

"I don't know if he would've gone that far."

"They've already shot at you."

"I just don't want to become like them. We can be better people. You know?"

Sandra squeezed his arm. "Okay. We'll call. But right now, let's keep moving. Whoever they are, they probably don't care about being the better people."

"Good point," Max said. They got back to their feet and headed along the street, their steps not filled with as much dread as before. Up ahead, the road ended. The grass rose steeply for just a short step and off to the right they saw a giant, silver coffee pot, at least ten-feet high, probably more, surrounded by flowers. "What the heck?"

A small plaque explained that the large tin coffee pot had been created in 1858 by the Mickey brothers as an advertisement for their tinsmith business. Max shook his head. "This place is nuts," he said.

"I think it's neat," Sandra said. "It's like a touch of the modern day seeping back into history. Granted, advertising isn't the best aspect of us to have seep back but still it just makes me ..."

"Are you okay?" Max asked. Sandra turned around and stared. Max followed her gaze and saw nothing. "Another ghost?"

She nodded. Then she whispered, "It's coming straight at us. It's beckoning us."

"Tell it to go away. We're done for the night."

"I can barely hear him."

"There's nothing worth hearing."

"Shush already."

Sandra leaned forward and cupped one ear. She looked so ridiculous, appearing to listen to the giant coffee pot, that Max felt another wave of giggles rising. But before he could utter one chuckle, Sandra stepped back with her face drained of color. A few months ago, Max would have said, "What's the matter? See a ghost?" Of course, now, he knew she had and that something far worse bothered her.

She turned her gaze toward him and said, "He says he's been watching us tonight. He says he knows what book we want. We just have to follow him."

"So, what's the matter?"

"We have to go over there," she said pointing further along the way they had been traveling.

"Why's that scare you? I just see trees and the street. Is there something else?"

"One more street over — that's where we're going."

Without offering more, she walked away. Max hurried to her side and attempted to get her to talk, but she behaved in a weird, zombie-like manner. *Shock,* he thought. But from what?

They passed a white building with tall columns that once may have been a mansion or a public assembly but now served as apartments. Turning up Bank Street, they saw sleek black statuettes lining the outside of the apartment building — a lion, a retriever, and some other dog Max did not know. The statuettes held relaxed poses that filled Max with more dread than if they had been menacing in appearance — as if their calm lay in knowing they had to exert such little effort to capture their prey.

"Where's it taking us?" Max asked, not expecting an answer but needing to hear a voice even if it belonged to him. He tasted blood in his mouth and swallowed it down. Sandra moved on, one hand out as if feeling for the ghost more than seeing the thing.

Bank Street rose steeply, and when they finally reached the next street over, Max huffed as he stared at the gothic structure. *A church,* he thought. Then he understood Sandra's behavior. Before them, stretching off into the distance was a low, brick wall with white fencing completing it. An arched gate led into an enormous field. A sign read:

SALEM MORAVIAN GRAVEYARD
"GOD'S ACRE"
1771
PLEASE BE REVERENT AND
RESPECTFUL OF THIS SPECIAL PLACE.

Chapter 22

WHEN THEY PASSED THROUGH THE ARCHWAY, everything changed. Until that moment, even as they crossed the street and approached the cemetery, Max would have been glad to call it a night. His body ached, his nerves jangled, nothing felt right. But when they entered the stone fields, though his fear compounded, his mind swelled with awe — never had he seen a cemetery like this one.

The graves were all the same — flat, white tablets laid in orderly squares; men and women separated; a few American flags the only vertical aspect to the burials. Enormous, ancient trees protected much of the well-manicured area.

Max figured that in daylight this would be a charming, peaceful place. At night, however, the eerie uniformity and stark whiteness of the tombstones mixed with the thick silence surrounding the cemetery created a stomach-twisting sensation. He felt burdened by the graves as if a giant child had placed them so carefully and now hawked over to make sure he did not disturb a single thing.

"There's too many," Sandra said, squinting in the dark. "I can barely see."

Max saw nothing but imagined well that his wife suffered from the many ghosts of a graveyard. He wanted to push her to find the one they had followed but kept silent. She didn't need him to bug her about the obvious.

"This way, I think," Sandra said, picking up her pace while shielding her eyes with her hand.

As they walked, Max read the name, dates, and epitaphs off several graves. From his research he recognized many of them. Joseph Harris (1821-1883) *The Lord is my Shepard.* William Whitt (1900-1923) *Innocence Taken Early Will Shine In Heaven.* Rebecca Burman (1818-1890) *A Light in Our Days.* Eve Hull (1750-1837) *Tucker Loved Her.*

Max paused to read the marker again. So Eve had chosen Tucker after all. Only something must have happened to bring her home. No way would the Moravians bury her here if she was still married to a magic dabbling sinner.

"Honey? Can you see the ghosts?"

Max looked up at Sandra, surprised to see the concern on her face. "No. Only Drummond. Why? What are they doing?"

"The one we're following — it stopped here."

With a nod to the grave, Max said, "That's why." He let out a long breath. "I suppose I'll be digging quite a lot tonight."

"Max," she said, a sudden tremble in her voice that tightened around Max's neck and shoulders.

"What's wrong?"

Stepping back with her hand gesturing to the air in front of Max, she said, "The ghost. It's reaching toward you."

"Tell it to stop."

"Stop it! Please," she said, her eyes glistening. "It won't listen."

A scraping, shuffling sound rolled in. They both peered back toward the street. A dark figure approached, dragging one foot behind, clearly disoriented but determined.

"It's him," Max said.

"Run. Go. This ghost looks mean. I think it's going to do something bad. I think —"

But Max did not move. He watched the emptiness before him, wondering what it wanted with him. Why bring him all the way out here and show him the grave, if it only had wanted to harm him? Why approach slowly, cautiously, if it only had wanted to attack? "It's okay, honey," he said, knowing he sounded weak and unsure. "I think it wants to help us some more."

"You can't see this thing. Run!"

Max heard the shuffling from behind and felt the air in front of him grow cold. *Don't be an idiot,* he thought. He turned away, reached for Sandra's hand, and pushed off his feet but running away did not occur. Instead, he felt ice break into the back of his skull.

"Max!"

He faced Sandra, and before he could wonder what had caused her ghastly countenance, he saw the ghost. It floated next to him, wore a suit, tie, and derby from the late-1800s. Its face had rotted away leaving behind a skull with bits of stringy skin hanging from its jaws like seaweed from an ancient wreck. And it had its hand thrust into Max's head. The cold spreading throughout Max's brain brought sharp flashes of pain.

"Stop it!" Sandra screamed at the ghost, but it did not budge. "Max! Max! What's it doing to you? Are you okay?"

Max looked back toward the man that had been pursuing them. As he turned his head, he saw the blinding light of thousands of ghosts. "I can see them," he said. "This hurts, but I can see them all."

As his ear began to freeze, Max tried to focus on the book. The ghost had helped them get this far, maybe this 'sight' it had given him was also meant to help. *Hurry,* his cold brain implored.

Awestruck by the multitude of transparent figures floating throughout the graveyard, Max could not stop gawking — even as the cold and throbbing pain reached downward toward his chest, even as the man bent on killing them came closer. Like a grand masked ball, there were people of all ages dressed in all forms of clothing from the eighteenth century to present day. A young couple strolled hand in hand as if on a Sunday afternoon. A bent man hugged another man with a loud welcome. They all moved with grace like swans in morning fog.

"Max!" Sandra said, snapping him back.

The book. He scanned the nearest ghosts, hoping one of them carried it. The hand stuck in his head pushed him to the ground so that he looked upon Eve Hull's grave. He started digging around the edges, the stone cold to the touch — or perhaps his fingers had just gone numb, he couldn't tell.

"Hurry," Sandra said, knelling beside him to help dig.

The ghost that held him tugged and pushed. Max ignored these encouragements — he moved as fast as he could and no amount of pressure from a ghost would change that. He glanced up at the approaching man. "Damnit," Max said, turning toward the ghost, the pain in his head firing high at the movement. "Instead of hurting me, get your friends to stop that guy."

As he turned back, he saw at least ten, maybe twenty, ghosts soar toward the man — arms outstretched. As they prodded the man, slipping their hands into his head, arms, legs, stomach, and chest, the man convulsed with each attack. He fought against this invisible assault, forcing himself several steps forward. More ghosts flew in creating a blinding white light centered on the man. In the end, he turned away and scuttled from the cemetery.

As Max turned back to the grave, the cold spreading

over his stomach, he saw a ghostly outline inside the grave next to Eve Hull's. It was a glowing rectangle — like a book. He opened his mouth but no sound came out. He pointed but Sandra did not see his shaking hand.

When he fell to his knees, she looked up. "Enough!" she said. "You're going to kill him. Let him go. We'll find the book. Just let him go."

The ghost turned its hand more and Max groaned. Sandra stood and with a sound colder than Max's body felt, she said, "Let go of my husband." When the ghost did not move, she pulled back a fist and smashed the ghost in the stomach. It fell back and disappeared but not before uttering a shocked cry.

With a gulp of air as if he had been drowning, Max doubled over. Warmth flushed his body and every nerve tingled as if it had fallen asleep. "How ... did you ... do that?" he said through gasps.

Sandra smiled with bewildered excitement. "I figured if they can touch us —"

Max looked around but now only saw darkness. "Is it still here?"

"Yes, but it doesn't seem to be doing much. They're all just standing around waiting. I think I've freaked them out a little."

"Come here. This grave. The book is here. That's what the ghost wanted to show us."

Exhausted, but excited as well, Max and Sandra dug around the edges of the stone. Their fingers dirtied with the muddy ground, but they did not stop. Sweat mingled with drizzle, but they did not stop. They had been through too much that night to stop over such minor matters as discomfort.

When they had dug beneath the stone, Max gripped it with the tips of his fingers and lifted. Straining, he pulled the stone from the sucking ground. Sandra grabbed on from the other side and pulled. The gravestone lifted a little bit, but its weight threatened to bring it right back down. With a low grunt, Max lifted harder, getting one foot underneath him and pushing upward. The ground emitted a loud slurp and the stone broke free, sending a wave of warm air upward. It smelled bad, but bad odors were among their least concerns.

Sitting in the middle of the mud square that marked where the stone had been was a wrapped package. Neither Max nor Sandra moved at first. Stunned by the simple object that had caused so much trouble, Max felt a wave of guilt rush over him like he had when he was a kid and broke the law by stealing a comic book. He looked around the empty cemetery, half-expecting to see the police come zooming in with flashing reds and blues.

"Take it," Sandra said. "Take it and let's get out of here."

Max snatched the package and tucked it under his coat to protect it from the drizzle. Like a child anxious to receive a reward, he hurried his steps, clutching the package close to his stomach, protecting it like a baby. It pressed against his skin with a warm touch and the smell of decay drifted toward his nose as they headed back.

Though both wanted to get to the car and leave Old Salem, they took a long route around to continue avoiding Main Street. A car drove by — the lonely sound of its motor in the quiet night reached them long after it had passed. When they arrived at the small Salt Street lot and saw their car sitting under the large tree where they had left it, Max felt both relief and worry. Sandra gripped his hand.

They stood across the street, watching the car, wondering if the man who had assaulted them watched it, too. With water dribbling off of Max's head, his body cold except for the warmth of a package torn from the grave, his bones aching from the night's exertions, part of him just wanted to walk home. *The hell with this moron.* But the idea of walking for miles, of taking hours before he could safely open what rested against his stomach, was more than he could stand.

"Damn," he said, walking to the car with a firm step and a defiant scowl. Sandra came behind, de-activated the alarm, and unlocked the doors before they reached the car.

Once inside, Sandra drove off, not waiting for either of them to settle in, put on a seatbelt, or even open the package. She let out a long sigh dotted with chuckling. Then she reached above, flicked on the interior light, and said, "Well, go on. Let's see if this was worth it."

With careful motions, Max produced the package and unwrapped it. A journal — a leather-covered journal. The smell of old age and forgotten times wafted over him as he opened it to the first page.

"Oh," he said.

"What?"

"This isn't Hull's journal."

"What? No. That can't be," Sandra said, her eyes welling.

"It's okay. Really. Maybe even better. This journal belongs to Stan Bowman."

Chapter 23

MAX SETTLED INTO HIS DESK CHAIR like an injured dog —
slow, cautious, and whimpering. Every bit of skin, muscle,
and bone throbbed. Every motion, every glance, every
sound pulsed pain through his head far exceeding the worst
hangover of his college life. Wrapped in a blanket while his
clothes dried over a chair, he sipped a little of the whiskey
Drummond had provided, turning his whimpers into less
embarrassing grumbles.

"Enough of your whining; what's in the journal?"
Drummond asked as he paced the room.

Sandra eased in the other dry chair, also wrapped in a
blanket, also sipping Drummond's whiskey. She leaned her
head back, closed her eyes, and would have fallen asleep if
not for her own intense curiosity over the journal.

Max yawned. It was close to four in the morning, and
his body reminded him for the hundredth time that night,
he was no longer a young man. All-nighters of any variety
were a thing of the past.

"Let's see," he said as he opened the journal. Its
distinctive, earthy odor lifted into the air as he turned the
pages. "You gotta be joking."

"What's wrong?" Drummond asked.

"No dates," Max said, skimming page after page. "Not a
single date is recorded. What kind of nitwit writes a journal

without dates?"

Sandra smiled. "The kind that only writes it for himself. I hate it when people date their entries as if expecting that someday when they die, the public will cry out to know about their lives and all that crap. Nobody cares about that stuff. He wrote this for himself. And that's good for us. It means we'll get the unvarnished truth as he saw it."

Drummond pointed to Sandra. "You are a bright, bright lady. I'm telling you, sweetheart, if you weren't married and I wasn't dead —"

"I'll keep that in mind."

"Here," Max said. "Yeah, listen to this one — 'It's been a long time since I've written in this thing. Part of me thought I was done with it. I thought I didn't need this old book anymore. Guess some things never finish. They just hang in the back of your head waiting for a chance to spring alive again. The war was like that. I'm done with it. Served my time, did a good job, and gave up good use of a leg in the process. Damn Krauts took my leg. And I'm thinking I'm finished, it's over for me, nothing more to do with it. But some things just never die. I don't think a single one of us will ever be done with this war. We'll be in our eighties, walking with canes, and we'll still be living the whole nightmare over and over. And to prove this, I merely have to think about today. Mr. William Hull dropped by with RJR himself. They walked in like two noblemen come to look at the serfs. For the first time in my life I thought I might know what a negro feels like. I think some others felt it too. Especially Artie Thompson. After the two kings left, one of the black boys who tries to pick up a few bit helping with trash and such came in. Artie hollered on and on, spit on the boy, and kicked him a few times until the tike ran off. But that's not the thing. The thing was Hull."

"Skip all this," Drummond said. "Somewhere in the

back there should be papers or drawings or something like this curse on the floor."

Max skimmed through the final ten pages. Then he went backward until he reached the spot he had read from. With a gentle shake of his head, he closed the book and said, "Sorry. It's not here."

"It has to be."

"This is Stan Bowman's journal. Your curse must be in Hull's or the witch's, if either of them even kept a journal."

"Damnit!" Drummond swiped his hand through the clothes drying on the chair, knocking a few to the floor.

Setting her mug on the desk with a hard thump, Sandra bent over to pick up the fallen clothes. She said, "Read some more. Bowman knew Hull, right? Maybe there's something in there that will help us find Drummond's —"

"That's right. She's right. Read more. Come on."

Max re-opened the journal, snapping the pages as he found his place. Drummond hovered behind, his eagerness wrapping around Max like a python. "A little space, please," Max said. Drummond muttered as he drifted toward the door. "Thank you. Now, here it is. 'The thing was Hull. I'd never met the man before today. I'd heard about him, of course, and like many big names, he did not match his celebrity. He struck me as a priss. To be fair, I didn't think too highly of him before any of today happened. He used his influence to avoid serving. How can you respect a man like that? Anyway, there he was acting as if he were better than the rest of us and he starts looking over the Krauts. And here's where today got real weird. I swear he recognized one of them. He doggone knew one of those Krauts for sure. I have no doubt. And the Kraut knew him. They locked eyes for just a second, but I saw it. So, the real question now is what do I do about it?'"

"Well, well," Drummond said. "I smell blackmail."

"You see the worst in everybody," Max said.

"Occupational hazard."

"'I called on Hull today. That must have given his staff a fit or two, crappy little nothing like me just walking up to his gate. They were all ready to throw me out but I told them they'd lose their jobs if they didn't see that William Hull read my letter. There was just enough conviction in my voice that they weren't sure what to do. So, they did what any fearful staff does — they hedged their bets. One took the letter to Hull while the other glared at me and waited for the merest sliver of a signal to pound me into the dirt. Less than five minutes later, I was sitting in Hull's office. The letter said that I saw the look between him and the Kraut. That was it. Simple and direct. I was nervous going in there. Not everyday you try to blackmail a multi-millionaire.'"

"Told you so."

Drummond's crowing rattled Max's ears, sending another splitting ache through his head. "Great," Max said. "You're gifted at predicting the evils within men's hearts. Can I continue now? 'I know it was a bad thing to do but we're just getting our feet back on the ground, and to give Annabelle more than just getting by money. To be able to buy her a nice coat or even (I can't believe I can even consider writing this down) to buy her jewelry, it's just too much to turn away. Besides, Hull don't need all that money. He can spare a little and still live like a spoiled king.' He goes on for a few pages ranting and cursing about Hull."

Max poured more whiskey in his mug. Drummond said, "Hey, go easy. That's all I have."

"You're dead, remember?"

"It's still mine. I like to have it around."

Turning the page, Max read on, "'Annabelle is asleep and I'm sitting here writing and in my coat pocket is a check for more money than I can even think about and now I'm saying the hell with all of them. I'm going to do what the government paid me to do for the last few years. Not exactly but close enough.'"

"Man," Sandra said, "this guy is a piece of work. He can justify anything. Blackmail, torture. What's next?"

With a far-off gaze, Drummond said, "Let's just hope he didn't write in detail about that. I've seen the end result of his handiwork. We can skip those details."

Sitting up in his chair, his drying hair matted against his forehead, Max said, "Listen to this: 'I've done it. The bastard Kraut is sitting here in front of me as I write this. I can't believe it. It was so easy. I rented this place with Hull's money, and nobody is going to bother us.' There's a break and then he writes ..."

"What? What does he write?" Drummond asked.

Max swallowed against his nausea. "Details," he said.

"Skip ahead."

"Please," Sandra added.

While Max tried to avoid various combinations of words like 'inserted the rod into his intestines,' Drummond resumed his pacing. Sandra said, "It's a good thing you're a ghost. We'd have no carpet left."

Drummond ignored her. "When I was on this case, we never were able to trace the money Bowman used to finance his torture chamber. Mostly he paid in cash, but this says he paid for it all with blackmail money, and that Hull gave the initial payment by check."

"So, how come there's no record?"

"And why did Bowman take a check at all? He's not brilliant but he never struck me as a dumb man. Why would he leave any kind of a paper trail?"

Sandra yawned. "Maybe he knew from the start there wouldn't be a paper trail."

"The bank," Drummond said. "I'll bet if we look a little deeper into Bowman's bank we'll find it was owned in some large part by William Hull. He could make the trail disappear with relative ease. Whatever was going on with that look, whatever was worth paying off Bowman to keep secret, Hull must have planned to fix the paper trail as well. And it's got to be far easier fixing it when the paper belongs to your own bank."

"He gets pretty nuts near the end," Max said as he turned another page. "It all becomes jumbled rambling. He thinks Annabelle is cheating on him. 'All the time I catch her looking away from me, wracked with guilt. And she stares at me too. She stares and stares and stares as if I'm going to jump up and yell that yes I am the man! I am the one! The scourge who has kidnapped and tortured five German POWs. Look on me with disgust, disdain, diswhateverthefuckyouwant! I am all you hate! So go off and fuck whoever you've got! But she'll get no satisfaction from me. And I'll find out, don't worry about that, I'll find out who she's seeing.'"

Sandra said, "Sounds pretty out there."

Drummond grunted. "You think she really was cheating on him? That'd be great."

"It would?"

"Well, not for him, but for us. Her lover might still be around. It's a lead."

"But we don't know who he is."

"Not yet."

"Wow," Max said. "Listen here: 'Hull came by tonight. I was chiseling out Günther's incisors and then there's Hull standing behind me. He blows on and on about how what I was doing was wrong. But he wasn't there. He never fought against these bastards. Money kept him from serving a day in the war. I got no money. My leg is worthless. But I got these POWs, so I'm not stopping. It's the only thing that gets me through the day. Hull said I'd go to Hell for all this. Probably. But I'm doing it anyway.' That's it. No more entries."

"He must've disappeared after that," Drummond said.

"Well," Max said, "at least you know what happened. Or most of it, anyway."

Sandra collected their mugs and cleaned them in the bathroom sink. "You know," she said, "I still don't understand why all this cursing business happened. So what if Drummond was closing in on Hull? There was no paper trail. Hull bought off Annabelle with a stock option. He covered his tracks except for this journal. Right? Whatever Hull's big secret was, he had buried it fine. And what does it matter now? I mean why was somebody trying to stop us tonight from finding this thing?"

"Honey," Max said as she stepped back into the office. Taylor leaned in the hall doorway, sopping wet, bruised and bleeding, and holding a handgun. "I think we're about to have an answer."

Chapter 24

SANDRA EDGED TOWARDS MAX. "You?" she said. "You're the guy that's been after us?"

"That just takes it all, don't it?" Drummond said.

Taylor ran his tongue over a bloody gap in his teeth. "You really think I was just some idiot lackey? You really think I just sat around all day waiting for orders from you? I've been working for Hull this whole time."

"Well, we knew that," said Max. "We just didn't think you'd be — what are you?"

"I'm a hitman," Taylor said, kicking at a chair and spitting out blood.

"More like a wannabe hitman," Drummond said as he floated behind Taylor and made goofy faces. The gun in Taylor's trembling hand persuaded Max not to laugh. Sandra, however, took a less tactful approach.

"So," she said, "you're a hitman? Hull hired you to kill us? I don't think so. I mean if that were true, we would've been dead awhile ago. You've been in this office for a long time. You had plenty of opportunities to do away with us."

"I was ordered to watch you."

"That I believe."

Taylor stepped forward, letting the gun lead him. "Shut up, bitch. I'm going to take care of you two and Mr. Hull will know then just who he can count on."

Max spoke up. "Hull doesn't know you're doing this?"

"I'm going to solve his problem with you."

"On behalf of my wife, I take back everything she said. You are a brave man." Max looked right at Drummond and tilted his head toward Taylor. Drummond contorted his face into another silly expression. "After all, you know better than us just how terrifying Hull can be. You know how powerful he is. And I'm sure you know how specific he is in his orders. Yet in spite of all of that, you're still willing to take this matter on yourself. You're making your own decision regardless of how it may go against Hull's wishes. That's seriously brave."

"He'll promote me, he'll be so happy," Taylor said, but doubt covered his face. Again, Max tried to signal Drummond, and this time Drummond looked in the direction Max nodded, then shrugged.

"If he's happy, you're absolutely right — probably. Of course, if you're wrong, if he had you watching us so that he could learn something important or maybe choose a specific moment to hurt us, then you've screwed things up for him. That's a ballsy decision you've made. I admire your willingness to take the chance."

Spitting more blood, Taylor said, "Stop that. You just shut up. I know what I'm doing. Hull needs good thinkers, good soldiers, and best is those who can do both. That's what I'm going to show him right now."

"You know, ghosts did that to you," Max said, once more trying to get through to Drummond. "In the cemetery, when you felt all those cold stabs of pain, those came from ghosts."

"What the fuck are talking about now? Just shut up."

"I'm merely saying that many people don't realize just how strong ghosts are, just how much they're able to interact with our world. People may think they can only move a piece of paper or a book, but they can cause real pain."

Drummond's eyes widened and a malicious grin rose from his lips. With a wink, he made a fist, pulled back, and punched Taylor hard in the ribs. Then everything went crazy.

Taylor squealed in surprise and dropped the gun. Drummond screamed and flew off clutching his hand. Sandra dove for the gun while Taylor looked upon his empty hand in shock. As Sandra picked up the gun, Taylor gained his senses and kicked her in the side. She rolled over seizing her ribs. At the same time, Max launched from his desk to tackle Taylor. The two men tumbled to the ground, grappling and punching while Drummond crouched in the corner wheezing.

"That hurt," he managed to say, but nobody bothered to listen. Sandra struggled for her own breaths of air while Taylor had managed to roll behind Max and get an arm around his throat. Max tried wedging his hand between his throat and Taylor's arm but the boy's grip was too tight. He tried elbowing Taylor, and though he made contact, the boy did not loosen his arm. Max's lungs burned at the lack of oxygen.

"I'm not such a peon now, am I?" Taylor said. "You think you can defy a great man like Hull? You think you can mess with his people? Well, I'm his people, and this is what you get."

When Max saw the ceiling light go dark, he figured the end had come. Then he heard a high-pitched cry and he could breathe again. Taylor shoved him over, and as he strained for air, he saw Taylor rolling on the ground clutching his groin. The ceiling light had not gone out — Sandra had blocked it when she stood and kicked Taylor.

Her sweet hands rubbed Max's back for a moment.

"You okay, honey? Can you talk?"

"I feel like dirt," Max managed.

"Me, too."

"Get the gun."

"I got it. Don't worry. Guess Taylor forgot to put on a new cup."

The way her sentence drifted off scared Max. He looked up. Mr. Modesto stood at the door, taking in the disheveled room.

Despite his pain, Taylor rose to his feet and bowed. "Mr. Modesto. I, well, I'm, um, that is —"

"Please be quiet," Modesto said in his rich tones.

"Yes, sir," Taylor said, looking younger with every second.

Modesto offered a hand to help Max, and with it came the rich scent of cologne. Max ignored the hand and, with Sandra's help, stood. "I think," Max said, "we can agree that Taylor should no longer be here."

"I think we are beyond that." Modesto lifted his right hand, and two men entered to escort Taylor away.

"Wait. What's going to happen to him? Don't hurt him."

"He tried to kill you."

"He tried to impress your boss."

"Your boss as well."

"Not anymore. I don't think that I can continue to work for him," Max said, and he could feel Sandra's tension grow.

"I see. Then I suppose I'll have to inform our employer. He will be disappointed."

"I'm sure."

"Of course, you'll no longer have access to this office."

"I only ask for a few days to pack up."

"That should be acceptable. And naturally, our files will remain with us, as will the journal you acquired this past evening."

"Journal?"

"You don't really believe I'll let you keep it, do you?"

Max considered his options and saw fairly fast that, unless he planned to attack Modesto, he had none at the moment. Attacking Modesto did not strike Max as a wise move — satisfying but not wise. Modesto stepped over to the desk, lifted the journal, and placed it in his briefcase, his movements always graceful, always controlled. Then he left, saying over his shoulder, "Good day, Mr. Porter."

"Why the hell did you do that?" Drummond said once Modesto had exited.

"What could I do? He knew we had the journal."

"Not the journal, you idiot. Why'd you quit working for Hull? Now you've lost this office. And that means I'm stuck here — still."

"Don't get mad at me. You didn't seem to be doing much good either."

"I've got a damn foot-long blade of fire cutting through my hand right now thanks to you."

"What are you talking about?"

"You're the one who told me to attack Taylor. Do you know how painful it is to hit somebody in the corporal world?"

"Like a foot-long blade of fire cutting through your hand?"

"I swear if it didn't mean more pain, I'd punch you in the jaw right now."

Sandra helped Max back into his chair. "Back off," she said. "Max has gone through a lot to help you out."

"Some help."

"He could've left you from day one. You'd be a bodiless spirit in the bookcase. He didn't have to do any of it."

"But he did do it, and now he's got my hopes up and

what's going to happen? Nothing. I'm given the short stick again."

"Sorry if I don't cry, but my husband has risked his life for you. Hell, so have I. And by quitting this job, our lives may be in even more danger."

"Exactly," Drummond said as if everything out of Sandra's mouth had supported his view. "Call Modesto and apologize for talking so rashly. Get your job back. Maybe Hull won't try to silence you if he thinks he controls you."

"Not likely," Max said.

"Then why'd you do it? I don't get it."

"Because I'm angry," Max said, pushing away at Sandra's fawning. "All that we went through tonight and the moment that ass walked into this office, I knew he'd be taking the journal. It's not fair. How are we supposed to do anything good in here when everything is stacked against us? It's like they brought us down here just to play with us, and I'm tired of it. I just want to go home, get some sleep, leave this place, and move on."

Drummond let out a defiant laugh. "You're only saying that 'cause Modesto showed up. Before that, when you'd thought you'd won the day, you were all smiles. I saw it. You like this. I know. I've seen that look many times — half of them while looking in the mirror. Let me tell you something, though. You can't win every day. Sometimes you've got to be humbled a little. The important thing is—"

"Will you shut up already," Max said.

"Hey, I don't deserve that from you."

Sandra threw a towel through Drummond. "Just leave him alone, already."

"I'm just saying that —"

To Sandra, Max said, "Please go home ... and start packing."

"Okay," she said, her disappointment obvious.

Max buttoned on his shirt and stormed out of the office. "I'm going for a walk," he said, ignoring the chill brought on by his shirt — still damp from the evening's excursion.

At least an hour passed, Max did not keep track, when he found himself rambling down Fourth Street for the umpteenth time. When he had started his walk, he was fed-up and anxious to go. However, after he had calmed a bit, he remembered the way Sandra had fallen in love with the area when they first arrived. And now he liked it a lot, too. Winston-Salem was more than just Hull, and he had to admit that he would miss some of this place. If only he had enough strength to turn away that carrot from the beginning. Of course, then he would never have come here. He and Sandra would be wandering somewhere in the Mid-West or the Northeast, struggling to build a life.

"Some life," he said — ghosts, witches, graveyards, curses, blackmail, and torture. Yet, the morning air smelled fresher than any he had experienced elsewhere. The people (except for those associated with Hull) were genuinely nice.

No, it's none of that. I'm just tired of disappointing Sandra. This move to the South was meant to be their fresh start — his new job, his chance to make it all right. *And it's all just crap, now.*

As the road inclined, Max noticed the sound of a car just behind him — not passing but following. He quickened his pace and tried to get a glimpse of the vehicle in the store window reflections. He saw a dented van with no specific markings. When he turned around the van slowed, inching forward with trepidation. The driver wore a mask. With a sudden motion, the van gunned forward, screeched to a stop in front of Max, and the side door slid open. Two masked men jumped out, grabbed Max, and pulled him inside.

Just got crappier, Max thought as the van drove off.

Chapter 25

A RICH AROMA — cinnamon and burnt incense. The odor was strong enough to wake Max. With the back of his head throbbing in time with his pulse, he opened his eyes. Wolves, bears, and hyenas glared back at him. Wood-carvings. He knew them, too. They were on a rolltop desk — the one that belonged to Dr. Connor.

He sat in a wooden office chair — his wrists and legs tied to its frame. Every muscle in his body complained, and his eyes threatened to close for a long, relaxing sleep. A man crouched nearby and a woman stood a few feet further away. "Modesto?" Max said, a grim, dry taste in his mouth.

"I apologize for the rather rough way you were handled, but I did not think you would have come here otherwise," Modesto said. He had removed his tailored jacket and his sleeves were rolled up like a harried newspaper editor from the 1940s. His disarray frightened Max more than anything else at that moment.

"I already gave you the journal."

"And I thank you."

Dr. Connor bent closer to him and said, "You were an easy one. We led you a little down the path and you went for the bait. I thought you'd have been tougher to wrangle, but —"

"That's enough," Modesto said. "I apologize for the

doctor as well. She's a little excited. We've been searching for this journal for quite some time. I had always suspected it was in the cemetery, but our employer has a lot of strong feelings when it comes to Moravian cemeteries. And then there was no way to find out which grave. Until we had you find it for us."

"What made you think I could do it?"

"We simply hired you to help us out. We figured that your information would aid us in our search. I never really thought you'd be the one to locate the journal. You've never shown yourself to be all that bright. So, this was just a bonus."

"This whole job was a setup to find that journal?" Max said. He was about to point out that it didn't contain Drummond's curse but held back. Instead, he added, "All this just to protect Hull? From what? A little embarrassment. The guy's dead now, anyway."

Modesto brought his face right in front of Max and studied him. Then he backed away and said, "I don't think he knows much more. We should be fine."

"Then ..." Dr. Connor said like a girl awaiting her turn for a pony ride.

"Yes. You may do with him as you like. Just make sure there's nothing left to find."

With a relieved shudder, she said, "Thank you." She handed Modesto his jacket. "If you need anything else, of course, I'm always here for you."

"We appreciate that."

"And I will take care of everything here. Don't worry."

"I never do," Modesto said and walked away.

Dr. Connor turned towards Max. "Let's see now. I still have a little of your blood and hair. What shall I do with it?" She took the seat Modesto had occupied and with a giddy laugh, she folded her hands in her lap. With exaggerated surprise, she said, "Oh, I know, I'll make a little spell you might be familiar with. It's called a binding spell."

Max stayed silent. He guessed that pleading would gain him nothing, and the idea of spending what little time he had left negotiating with this awful person (let alone begging) did not sit well. Instead, while Dr. Connor mashed various plants in a wooden bowl, Max scanned the room for anything that might help.

She had a number of sharp implements — some obvious like knives, some less so like a hooked item that reminded Max of a dentist's pick. The remnants of rope from what they had used to tie him had been piled on the floor. Three candles burned in an ornate holder sitting on the desk. However, nothing could be considered useful unless he got out of the chair.

"Can I ask you something?" Max said, trying to go with his gut like Drummond.

"You can ask. I don't guarantee I'll answer."

"Your grandmother — why did she bind Drummond? I know what you said last time, but seeing as I won't have time to get Drummond to talk with you, I'm just curious. Was it just a lover's revenge?"

After placing another ingredient in the bowl and stirring it up, she said, "A little revenge, yes. I don't think she was too mad at him, though. She was a wise woman and knew what sleeping with a man like Drummond meant."

"Then it was something else?"

Dr. Connor sniffed the bowl and reeled back. "That's about right. Maybe a little more of your blood just to be safe." She walked behind him, and for a second Max thought she would slit his throat. She laughed at his tensed body. "Not yet. You don't die until the end, when your soul gets bound to this chair. Then I suppose I'll put the chair on the curb. Let whoever wants it, take it. Or perhaps the garbage men will take it away and you can haunt the dump forever. For now, I just need this." With a hunting knife, she made a thin cut in Max's bicep and let his blood drain into the wooden bowl. "That's better."

"So, why bind Drummond when killing him off would have worked better?"

"That was the backup plan."

"Backup? Why would she need a backup plan? Unless, you mean, she didn't know if it would work?"

"My grandmother was a fantastic witch. Just because Hull didn't trust her doesn't mean she would ever have failed. And the proof is haunting your office."

"But if —"

With the back of her hand, Dr. Connor struck Max. "Be quiet now."

Using the blood-soaked mixture from the bowl, she drew a circle around the chair. All the time, she chanted. Max could not understand the language she used. The pungent fumes encircling him and the non-stop chanting flamed the pressures mounting inside him. He hated it, but he could feel tears welling.

Before he could control himself, he blurted out, "Please, don't do this. I don't know anything important. This is just a big mistake. Please —"

With a sadistic grin, Connor gazed up at him. She never stopped chanting. She never stopped drawing her circle.

Drummond went through this, Max thought. He saw it as if it were a live performance before him — Hull's witch performing this same spell, binding Drummond to his office; the incessant chanting; the desperation boiling inside. *No wonder Drummond's so pissed off all the time.*

"Okay, then," Dr. Connor said as she stepped back. Max thought he saw a little sadness, pity perhaps, creep into her eyes as she appreciated her work.

"Dr. Connor?" a voice called from behind.

Dr. Connor scowled as she stepped by Max. He heard a door open. "What is it?"

"Mr. Kenroy's insurance company is on the phone."

"Again?"

"They're disputing last May's charges and they wish to talk with you."

"Tell them I'm busy and that —"

"I'm sorry, Doctor, but they're insisting. They said this is the fifth time they've called, and they threatened if you didn't talk with them —"

"Fine, fine. I'll be right there. Oh, and tell Mrs. Johnson she'll have to wait until tomorrow for those curses. My schedule got a surprise booking today."

Max waited. He could feel her watching him, feel her pondering what to do, and finally, he heard her close and lock the door with a huff.

He struggled against his restraints with no success. The idea of hopping to the exit came and went — she would hear, and besides, it was a stupid thought. What would he do once he got there? Hop to freedom?

He fought to move his legs. His right foot had just a tiny bit of mobility. Looking down, he saw the tip of his foot moving right near the edge of the binding circle.

Perhaps ...

Wiggling his foot back and forth, he inched the chair closer to the circle but still could not reach it. Muffled sounds of Dr. Connor arguing over the phone reached Max's ears. He took a deep breath and pushed again with his foot. This time the tip of his shoe touched the powdery substance. Again, wiggling his toe, he made a small break in the circle then worked his way back to his original position.

It would have to do.

He did not know for sure if breaking the circle would

have any effect on the spell, but he now knew magic and spells were real — so why not other things he had heard growing up? Wasn't that the way magic circles worked? Break the circle and the spell failed. He hoped so, because even if he had come up with another idea, it was too late. He heard the phone slam down, and a moment later, the door opened.

As Dr. Connor walked by, she slapped Max in the back of the head. She knelt down in front of him and the circle, flustered but regaining her composure. Max used every ounce of will power not to look at the break in the circle. Each motion of her head jangled his nerves.

After several deep breaths, she began to chant again. She lit a stick of incense and held it above her head, then made small motions with it over the edge of the circle. "Good-bye," she said, raising her eyes toward Max with a look both seductive and repulsive. Then she dropped the burning incense onto the powdered circle.

In the fraction of a second before the explosion, Max saw confusion, fear, and resigned understanding pass over Dr. Connor's face. Then the blast hit. White light splashed from below and intense heat pushed upward. As Max flew backwards, still tied to the chair, he saw Dr. Connor grasping her face and screaming as the powerful waves shoved her flat.

The chair broke through the thin, office wall and pulled Max with it. When he hit the hard floor of the broom closet, the chair shattered, as did his right wrist. Despite the tumultuous noise of the explosion, he heard his bones breaking. Then a mop clattered on his head.

A few seconds passed before he could stand. Holding his right hand close to his chest, he checked the rest of his body for injuries. Just scratches. A hesitant knocking came from the office door.

"Dr. Connor?" the assistant asked. Her meek voice would have been comical if Max had not come close to losing his life only moments before. "Are you okay?"

Stepping through the wall (an effort of sheer will considering the pain in his legs), Max saw Dr. Connor sprawled on the floor, face down, smoke whirling through her hair. Fine with him. He stumbled toward the back exit (one he thought he had become too familiar with already) and walked into the parking lot. The morning sun blazed in the sky.

He headed toward the chain stores figuring public places would keep anybody from moving on him for awhile. His wrist cried out for the emergency room. With his good hand, he checked his pocket — still had the cell phone.

Flipping it open, intending to call Sandra for help, he froze. *One missed call,* the phone displayed. He tried to convince himself that the trepidation he felt worming through him was only a result of the stresses he had endured in the last two days. The phone call could be from anyone about anything. Yet as he pressed the button to play the voicemail, the feeling intensified.

"Um, Mr. Porter, this here is Sam. I've found the names of those hoods that attacked you. That is, their real names." As Max listened to Sam speak the second name, everything changed.

Chapter 26

LEANING AGAINST HIS CAR across the street from the South Side home he had come to know better than he had ever expected, Max finished wrapping his hand. Although he felt the pressure of time upon every moment, the pain in his hand forced him to stop at the nearest drugstore on his way to this house — that and the insistence of his wife. Now, as he looked upon the dusty Chevy in the driveway and smelled stale flowers in the air, he worried he had made a mistake. The fact that Annabelle Bowman was more involved in all this came as no surprise — Max's alarm grew from not knowing where her loyalties fell.

"Keep the car running," he said to Sandra. "I'm not very welcome here."

"I'll add it to the list."

"Cute, honey."

"Just be careful."

Max approached the house, forcing confidence into his unsure demeanor. As he reached the porch, Annabelle opened the front door. She pointed a crooked finger at him, her red face scrunched in anger.

"I told you not to come back. Now get the hell away," she said, spit flying from her small mouth.

"I'm sorry. I don't want to upset you —"

"Then go."

"— but we have to talk."

"I'm going to call the police."

"Just a few minutes and I'll go."

"You go," she said and turned away. "I'll get Stan's shotgun."

"I know about Stephen."

When Annabelle turned back, her face had fallen and her color drained. Part shock, but Max saw fear, too.

"I just need a few answers. Then I'll go. Please."

For a blistering moment, Max thought she might faint or simply go catatonic. Instead, she walked deeper in her house, pushing the door slightly open as she left. Max took this as an invitation.

As he entered, he heard Annabelle call from the kitchen in a soft, dead voice, "Sit down, please. You know where."

He went to the small living room and settled on the overstuffed couch he had occupied in the past. Annabelle had the heat on, blowing hard from dusty vents. The hot air, thick with perfume, pressed on him. He wished he could open a window, get some of the cool, Fall air blowing inside, but he did not plan to be there too long — he could endure. When Annabelle arrived, she carried a tray with two glasses of scotch. She drained one glass in three gulps, set it down, and nursed the second glass.

"What do you want to know about my grandson?" she asked.

"How long were you having an affair with Hull?"

She choked a little on a sip of scotch. "Affair? I wasn't having an affair. And certainly not with that bastard. I hate Hull and all of his people."

"But Stephen's father was born several months after Stan's disappearance, Stan was convinced you were having an affair, and you received a hefty payoff in stock from Hull."

"Stephens father is Cal, and Cal is Stan's son."

"But why did —"

"Young man, shut up, please, and let me talk. You'll get more of what you want that way. Close the mouth and open the ears — my mother often said that and if nothing else, she was right about that one."

"Yes, ma'am," Max said, shrinking a bit in his seat.

After another sip of her drink, Annabelle said, "When Stan came back from the war, he never was the same. Whatever happened over there haunted him every single day. He never talked about it. Not once. But this tension always simmered right beneath the surface.

"And then came that day at work with Hull. The change in him was instant. He obsessed over those POWs and Hull and though he tried to keep it all away from me, I had figured out he planned to blackmail Hull. Well, things didn't go quite as he expected but I guess you know a lot about that by now. And if you don't, well, it doesn't really matter.

"I had become pregnant with Stan's child. Stan, sadly, had lost all sense of reality. The pressure of what he was doing to those POWs and Hull and memories of the war, I suppose they would call it Post Traumatic Stress nowadays. Back then, shellshock, if they bothered to diagnose it at all. For me, he was paranoid. And I knew he thought I was cheating on him, so I didn't dare tell him about being pregnant. He probably would have killed me. But I swear I was never unfaithful. I loved that man, and that boy is his."

"So when he went missing, he didn't know?"

"Never. He died not knowing about his son."

"Isn't it possible he's still alive? The police never found him."

Annabelle shot back the rest of her drink, then shook her head. "I watched him die — completely mad. I knew where he was hiding, and I tried to bring him back to me, tried to talk him into reality again, but it was too late. He took a shotgun and killed himself right before my eyes. Another week and I would have been showing enough for him to see. Maybe that would've changed his mind. Who knows? Maybe that would have made him turn that gun on me."

"I'm sorry."

She shrugged. "I cleaned it all up and buried him, and nobody will find him because nobody's really looking anymore."

"You had Stan's journal," Max said, the realization hitting him with surprising force. "That's why Hull bought you off."

"With all the police and media attention, he didn't dare harm me. So, he bought my silence, and I hid the journal. That should have been the end of it all. But my son, Cal, grew up to be a defiant child. Even from an early age he fought every rule I tried to lay down. When he hit his rebellious teen years, he went for the jugular — he started working for Hull."

"Shit."

"Don't swear in my house."

"Sorry. What happened?"

The skin below her right eye quivered as she looked into her past. "I tried to stop him, but he was a teenager and very much like his father. When Stan set his mind to something, no matter how insane, he could not be stopped. Cal had more than a touch of that in his blood.

"At the time I was furious, and though I couldn't stop him, I demanded he do one thing for me. I can still hear his impatient 'What?' but I held firm. He was to change his name, make sure Hull could not find out who he really was. I told him frankly that if Hull knew he was Cal Bowman, he would end up dead. That much got through. He changed his name. Later, he married and had Stephen. That's the name I've always known my grandson by. Stephen Bowman."

"And Stephen works for Hull, too?"

"Like many surrounding Hull, Cal died under questionable circumstances. But nobody bothered to look into it. So, Stephen picked up where his father left off."

Half to himself, Max asked, "Why would Hull put his own men in prison? Surely not for me. That makes worse sense than anything I've heard yet."

"Hull put Stephen in prison to keep an eye on him and to punish him for acting on his own accord."

This perked Max's attention. "He wasn't supposed to attack me, was he?"

"No. He did that to protect me and his secret. And it was a stupid thing to do. I can take care of myself. Besides, it sparked Hull's interest. He still doesn't know for sure who my grandson is, but I think he's starting to become concerned."

"So he puts him in jail."

Putting her glass on the table with a loud clack, she said, "You are a noisy fool. Now, for the last time shut up. Okay, then. See, my son, my darling little Cal, he didn't want to worry me with what his real motives were. All this time, I had felt betrayed, and it hurt him so bad but he knew he had to do it that way. If Hull ever found out who he was, Hull would come to me and he would see how angry I was and he would think Cal was truly on his side. But he wasn't. Cal wanted to find Hull's journal. That's what he was after the whole time. He wanted to find out what really happened between Hull and Stan."

Max's muscles tensed as he held his breath. "He found it," he whispered.

"No. That's why his son, my grandson, Stephen took over. And bless his heart, he succeeded."

"They really were looking for that journal."

"Yes. Your finding Stan's journal was a mistake. How did you find it anyway?"

A cold, painful thrust of memory spiked the back of Max's head. "I had some unusual help."

"That's all there is. Now, you know my dirty secret. Please, don't tell Hull. For my grandson."

"I won't, but I need you to do something for me."

Annabelle's face turned cold. "What is it?"

"I need you to call Stephen, arrange for him to meet me. I need to talk with him."

"You don't need me to visit the prison."

"I doubt he would talk with me. He tried to kill me."

"He wouldn't have really killed you. He just tried to scare you away from me."

"Look, I've listened to or read so many sides to this story, and I want the last one. Please."

Annabelle frowned as she looked out the window. "Okay," she said. "I'll do it. But go now."

Max checked the window — a green Ford and a grey Honda had pulled up; the Honda in the driveway and the Ford in front of the house.

"I'm sorry," Annabelle said. "I called Hull before I opened the door. I didn't know you were on my side."

"Is there a back door?"

With a nod, she pointed the way. "I'll call Stephen. He'll be waiting."

As he hurried down the hall, Max wondered how much more abuse his body could take. His hand throbbed non-stop, his muscles complained from the previous night, and his head ached with the feeling of ten hangovers. He moved like an elderly man as he negotiated the stairs to the backyard.

When he slid to the side of the house, he could hear Annabelle at the front door. "It's all okay, gentleman. He's gone now. I'm sorry to have bothered you. I'm just a foolish old lady."

The men said something too soft for Max to hear. Then Annabelle continued, "Come in, please. Have a drink. Oh, well, then have a seat. Let me see, he barged in here, very rude, and forced me to sit over there ..."

While she proceeded to fabricate a tale, Max crouched and duckwalked toward the front. He peeked onto the porch. Nobody. Both men were inside. He looked at both cars. No drivers waiting. Finally, he checked out his car. No Sandra.

Looking up and down the street, he sought her with fear rising in his throat. As his gaze passed over the car again, he saw movement — her hair. She was scrunched down in the driver's seat.

Relief swept Max as he rushed down the sidewalk several houses before crossing the street and then working his way back to the car. When he opened the passenger side door, Sandra jolted and stifled a yelp. She motioned him to stay down but get in, and before he could close the door, she hugged him. Wiping at her eyes, she pulled the car out and drove off in a casual manner though Max could see her pulse pounding on her neck. Pride took over and he kissed her cheek.

"Where to?" she asked.

"The prison. It's just a few blocks north."

Chapter 27

MAX SAT IN THE FUNCTIONAL WAITING ROOM, his elbows on his knees, trying to ignore the sideways glances he received from the other visitors. Fluorescent lights turned everything pale. He knew he looked awful — dirty, smelly, bruised, and broken. At least he had Sandra sitting next to him — that made him look less crazy. *Just a little longer,* he promised himself.

"Samuels," a guard called out, and a young, overweight lady went to see her boyfriend.

Each minute that passed by left more questions for Max to plague his weary brain. *What if Annabelle was still with Hull's men? What if she couldn't get Stephen to agree to see him? What if she had lied and was informing Hull of everything right this moment? What if* ... But Max knew that worrisome thoughts would not help him now. The time for over-cautious analysis had ended long ago. He had tested Drummond's way more than once, but now he had entered Drummond's world in full — a gut-reaction and from-the-hip world.

"Spanitti," the guard called out and waited as a woman assisted an old man into the visitor's room.

"I'm sorry, you know," Sandra said.

"For what?"

"The only reason we came down was because of me."

Despite the pain, Max shook his head. "No, no. Don't

start that. We came down here together. I screwed things up back in Michigan, I'm the one who couldn't bend a little for my boss to make it work, I'm the one who stole, and—"

"And I'm the one who found this job."

"What?" A chill covered Max, reaching all the way into his wrapped hand.

With her hands clutching her purse, Sandra said, "I wanted us out of Michigan, out of that mess, and I wanted you to feel better, confident — maybe even a bit arrogant like you were when we first met. So I started checking around on the Internet. I found out about this opportunity with Hull, but they didn't actually take job applications. You simply recommended somebody and they said they would look into it if they had an opening, and so, I recommended you."

Max brushed away the tears dribbling down her face. "I don't know what to say. I don't know whether to be mad or flattered or what."

"You can be all of those. Obviously, the plan didn't work out quite the way I had intended."

"Obviously." Max tried to put this new information in place, but it wouldn't fit. "Why even tell me this? What good is it?"

"I'm trying to be truthful. All the little secrets we keep hidden to protect each other, it only ever hurts us. You said we can't lie anymore, and you're right. I know you're mad. I can see it building up, but just know, I did it all out of love. And I'm sorry."

Sniffling, Sandra lowered her head. Max put his arm around her, and the warmth of her body against him was the first good sensation in quite some time. He squeezed her shoulder and kissed the top of her head.

"Porter," the guard called, but Max didn't want to let go of the moment.

As if reading his thoughts, Sandra said, "Go ahead. It's okay. I'll be right here when you're done."

Max followed the guard to a desk where he filled out some papers. Then he was taken to a large room teeming with inmates in orange jumpers, all seated with their loved ones, all talking in hushed, urgent tones. Near one of the wide, frosted windows, Max saw a man seated alone. The guard pointed and nodded.

Stephen Bowman shared a few of his grandmother's attributes — a similar nose and jaw. The eyes were Annabelle's as well. The rest of him came from Cal and Stan and whoever was his mother — harsh and angular. He had shaved his head, and Max noted the knife tattooed on the back of his hand.

"I'm letting you know right now," he said with a force that spoke of more time in prison than just this most recent stay, "I'm only seeing you because my Grandma asked me to. I got no care what happens to you, so long as it don't come down on me or her."

"Fair enough," Max said, sitting in a plastic, blue chair on the opposite side of a small table.

"So what do you want?"

"Your side of this twisted story, and, depending on what you say, maybe we can help each other out."

"Yeah, sure. My side. Listen, man, there are no sides, just the one truth."

"And what's that?"

"The fact is that Hull screwed over my whole family. He took a good, honorable man, a soldier who fought bravely for this country, and he fucked with his head until the guy couldn't think straight anymore and he did it to protect his own ass. Then when it all went to shit, he bought off my Grandma and walked away as if nothing happened."

"That's not quite the story I've heard."

"Well, you don't have what I have, do you?"

Max tried to stay calm. "You have Hull's journal?"

"You know I do. Why else would you be here talking with me? I'm guessing you figured it out the minute you knew who I was. Well, maybe not that fast. You had to check with my Grandma first. Then, you knew."

"I had a hunch you had something on Hull, but I never thought you had his journal."

"Well, you ain't getting it."

"I didn't think I would. But I do need to know what's in it. It's important to both of us. I mean, if I could find out who you are, then Hull will have no trouble finding it out, too. He just has to decide to look."

"That's the thing, though, he doesn't want to look. He's got no reason to doubt me and start looking."

Max gestured around them. "He put you in prison for attacking me. You don't think that'll get him curious about you? Make him wonder why you'd want to hurt me? Besides which, doesn't he know his journal is missing?"

"Of course, he does. He hired you, didn't he?"

"I don't know which journal he wanted me to find."

"Fact is, I joined up with Hull so I could get his journal. That's it. I mean, I didn't know it at the time. Back then, I just knew I wanted to hurt the bastard who hurt my family, took my father and Grandpa Stan from me. Understand? I figured I'd get in and just keep my eyes and ears open and one day, I'd find my opportunity. That's what I was waiting for. A gold opportunity.

"And it happened. Sitting in a bar, listening to college kids playing trivia games, just minding my business. And then I hear this guy boasting loud right next to me about how he knew the Hull family. Good friends, he says. Made a couple of rude comments about the lady Hulls, got himself some laughs. Right then, I decided I'd beat the guy to a pulp. Get myself some points with Hull. I sat there for two hours listening to this jerk go on and on. I swear he just wouldn't shut up.

"Around one in the morning, he finally leaves and I follow him to his car. Then I start bashing him and kicking him and he starts pleading with me. He's crying right there. I say some cool shit about Hull, and he looks at me hard. Like his whole face changed and he became Mister Cool for just a few seconds. And he says to me, 'You want something to really give you power?' He tells me about the journal. Turns out this fool was one of Hull's little gophers awhile back and he saw the journal. Hull found out and fired his ass.

"I thanked him for the info and then beat him some more," Stephen said with a grin.

Max checked the clock — high on the wall, protected by metal bars. He couldn't recall how long the guard had said he would have but knew time would run out soon enough. "So, you've got the journal now?"

Stephen pushed Max's chair with his foot. "It wasn't easy like that. It took planning, cunning, some real smart work. But yeah, I got it."

"Have you read it?"

"Not much else to do around here."

"And?"

"And Hull was a dick just like I thought," Stephen said, his face reddening as he puffed up his chest. A guard at the door looked over, ready to pounce if Stephen grew any more agitated. Stephen waved at the guard and formed a twisted smile. Then he lowered his voice and said, "When Grandpa Stan went to Hull to blackmail him, do you know what really happened? He refused to pay. He said nobody blackmails a Hull. Then he turned the whole thing around. He offered my dad all the blackmail money plus more if my dad would do a small job."

"The POW," Max said.

"Damn right. He wanted a specific one, Günther Scholz, and he wanted it covered up well, so he used Grandpa Stan's nuttiness against him. He paid to have the POWs captured and tortured. Just three of 'em. The one he wanted and two he didn't even know. But Grandpa Stan still struggled with the war and all, and this whole thing just snapped him. He hurt way more than just three. And, of course, he took his life, too. It's all laid out in that journal."

"Are you sure about that name. Günther Scholz?"

"Yup. That's the name. Strange thing, though. Hull gloats about all of this, except he doesn't say why that one POW made a difference anyway. I mean who was this dude who was so damn important that Hull had to screw Grandpa Stan over, wreck my family's life, and send me on a path that led here?"

"I don't know," Max said, but he kept trying to recall the names he had seen on that transfer slip. He thought Günther was not on it. An idea had formed that he suspected might be right; however, with the remaining time, he had a more urgent line of thought to pursue. "I'm going to try to help us both out here."

"Oh, are you?"

"Listen to me, please. You are not in a safe position just because you have the journal. But you can be. Together we can guarantee our safety."

"Nobody's safe, man. Nobody," Stephen said with an all-knowing smirk on his face. "You find some way to get rid of Hull, there'll be some other bastard taking his place. Fuck, our own government is the worst one of all. At least with Hull, I know who I'm dealing with."

"That's fine, if it's just you. But your Grandma is involved in all this, too."

Stephen's mouth tightened into a thin line. "You stay away from her."

"I'm not trying to bother her, but like you, I've got to protect those I love. And right now, you and her are standing in my way. But we can do it all different. The problem for both of us is Hull. So, if we work together, we can solve our problem."

"I'm listening."

"I need something that's in that journal. Not the journal, itself. I promise I won't take that from you. In fact, it's in both our interest for you to keep hold of that. But I do need a page, a single page."

Chapter 28

THE GREEN FORD IDLED just outside the prison. As Max and Sandra exited, its driver straightened and woke the man next to him. Max, however, did not head for his own car. This time, he walked straight toward the Ford. He thought they might drive away, but the closer he came to them, the more he understood that they were no longer trying to hide their interest in him. The driver's side window rolled down, and Max saw a muscular man who would have looked right at home in the prison Max had just left.

"Mr. Porter," the man said as he exhaled cigarette smoke, "we've been looking for you."

Max peered in the car and saw the other man, this one chubby but strong. "I want you to deliver a message to Modesto," Max said, impressing himself with his sturdiness of voice.

"Tell him yourself. We're here to escort you and your wife to see Mr. Modesto."

"No."

The chubby one unbuckled his seatbelt. "Looks like I get to do something after all."

Max knew he had only a few seconds left before these fools would stuff him in the car. "I have what Modesto wants. You guys try to hurt me or my wife, and he'll never get it. Tell him now. Call him up. You can see I'm not running. Heck, I'm the one who approached you, right? So, call him. Tell him I want to meet with him."

Chubby, his hand on the door, looked to Smoker for guidance. Smoker drummed his fingers on the steering wheel while he strained his gray matter. "Okay. Jack's going to help you wait, though, just in case you change your mind."

With more relish than he should have displayed, Jack, the chubby fellow, opened the car door, walked around the front, and stood behind Max and Sandra with his arms crossed over his chest. Sandra inched closer to Max, and her presence gave Max a slight comfort. He hoped he offered her some peace as well.

Smoker flipped open a cell phone and made the call. Less than a minute later, he said, "Okay, Porter, what do you want?"

"Tell him to come to my office in about two hours. We'll deal then."

Smoker relayed the message. "Done. Mr. Modesto wanted me to assure you that if for any reason you fail to deliver what you say you have or you try to run, the order to bring you in unharmed will be rescinded."

"I kind of figured that."

"And we're still going to be following you."

"I kind of figured that, as well."

"Don't try anything stupid."

"No, I won't. I'm just going to the library to do some last minute research. Then we're going to the office to meet your boss. That's it."

As Max and Sandra walked back to their car, Max kept calm. Sandra, however, had enough agitation for them both. "What are you doing? You don't have anything to give him."

"Honey, trust me. I've got this one covered."

Chapter 29

UPON ENTERING THE OFFICE, Max discovered a thrilled ghost, bubbling and chatty. It was the most frightening experience Max ever had with Drummond.

"Thank goodness you're okay," Drummond said and he flew around the room with nervous energy. "I mean I knew when you called Sandra that you were okay, but after they took you, well, I just started thinking about all of this and how I really got you involved and all that. I'm sorry. Really. I don't want you getting killed on my account. Oh, crap, look at your hand. They tortured you. I tell you if I wasn't stuck in this room, I'd be right out there helping you out. I mean it. I think you're okay, and I'm telling you, you need to have some backup. You can't go charging into a criminal's home —"

"Drummond," Max said. "Be quiet."

"That's a real nice thing to say. I'm just trying to let you know I was concerned and you're putting me down."

"Modesto's on his way," Max said. To Sandra he added, "Help me move this desk."

"Modesto?" Drummond said. "Why's he coming? The bastard already took the journal."

The desk scraped the floor, making a grating, high-pitched tone, but they managed to get it pushed toward the back wall. The binding curse marking the floor could now be seen in its entirety. In the center of the circle the four-headed snake bared its bloody mouth. The creature looked in all directions, promising to see all things at all times. It was disturbing, and Max tried to put it out of his mind even as he walked over the image.

"What's going on?" Drummond asked.

"We need to clean up as much as possible. I don't want anything that could be used as a weapon sitting around."

As Sandra picked up a few items, the old Drummond tones returned. He stood in front of Max, and said, "What the hell are you doing cleaning up for Modesto? You're not making any sense. What happened to you?"

"I need a lighter," Max said.

Sandra looked around in her purse. "I haven't got one."

"Drummond, is there a lighter in here or matches?"

"You tell me what I want to know, and I'll tell you what you want to know."

With the same strong tone he had used with the men in the green Ford, Max said, "If you want be stuck in this office for all eternity, then keep standing in my way."

"Fine," Drummond said and with a petulant grimace, he pointed to the bookshelf. "The book next to the one with the whiskey — two cigars and matches."

"Thank you. Now, relax," Max said as he retrieved the matchbox and placed it on the desk. "Everything's going to be fine."

"Then tell me —"

"No. Not you. Not even Sandra. I don't want Modesto even getting a hint of what I've done or what I'm going to do until I tell him."

"Son of a bitch, you've got something on him, don't you? You're going to stick it to him."

"Just be here and be ready."

"I ain't going anywhere, and I'm always ready."

Max let the comment stand as he wiped down the desktop. "Watch the window. Let us know when he arrives."

"Will do," Drummond said, his excitement palpable.

Using every last drop of strength, Max attempted to maintain a positive, confident, and winning attitude, though he knew the coming moments might hold the highest risk of anything he would ever do. If Modesto called his bluff, the whole thing would end with their deaths. He had no doubt. But he also believed the bluff was just powerful enough, with just enough proof to give it merit. They had a truly good chance of making it work out.

"He's here," Drummond said.

"Damn, he's early."

Sandra said nothing as she sped up her cleaning. "You can stop," Max said. "This'll have to do. You just stand back there, lean against the wall, and trust me."

"I do," she said. "If I look worried, it's not because I don't trust you. It's because I can see on your face just how dangerous whatever you're planning is going to be."

"I'm only going to talk. Lay out a few facts, and nothing more. Modesto's a logical man. He can understand basic reasoning."

Before any more words could be exchanged, Max saw Modesto's silhouette grow in the door's frosted glass. The door opened and in walked Modesto. He looked awful. Wrinkles marked his shirt as being at least a day old, his skin glistened with sweat, and the pressure Hull had placed upon him registered in the deep lines on his face. He also looked determined — this meeting would be the end, his eyes said. That stern gaze, more than anything else, gave Max both hope and fear.

Max watched Modesto, ready for any threat. At length, Modesto said, "Are we just going to stand here, or do you plan on telling me what you want for the journal?"

"You found Hull's journal?" Drummond asked.

"I don't want anything for the journal. I'm not giving it to you."

Modesto noticed a spot on his shoe, bent down, and rubbed at it. "You really are an idiot. I always thought you were just being blinded by greed or love for your wife or something normal like that, but to stand here and start playing this kind of game with a man like Mr. Hull — you're a fool."

"You don't think I know him? Let me tell you a few things. See, even after I'd put together most of the pieces of Stan Bowman's unfortunate final years, it wasn't until a little bit ago that I finally got it all."

"And now you think you know everything."

"I know enough. I know all about how Hull was responsible for driving Stan insane, how he pushed Stan to torture those POWs, and how he bought off Annabelle's silence. That's nothing new to you, though. But a few things gnawed at me. Why, for example, did you really hire me? How was I connected to all this? And why did you help me get those boys arrested when you had to have known that one of them was Stephen Bowman?"

Drummond's mouth formed an O, and he said, "Who the hell is Stephen Bowman?"

"I can understand," Max continued, "how Hull might've overlooked Bowman — just another cog in his machine. But the idea that you might? There's no way you would hire anybody for Hull's company without doing a thorough check. You knew that kid was Stephen Bowman. But I'm getting ahead of myself."

"May I sit?" Modesto asked as he noticed Sandra standing in the back.

"No," Max said. "The first question that we have to

address is why did Hull want those POWs tortured. It's perhaps the most crucial question because everything else, including me, flows from that. See that's what I missed at first. I was too busy dealing with the details that I forgot the bigger questions. You'll have to forgive me, though. I'm new to this side of things."

Drummond snorted. "Savor this moment, pal. I can tell the way you're talking, you've got something on him. Savor this. It's this very moment that always made my job worthwhile."

Taking a few steps closer, Max went on. "The bigger questions. That's what this is about. And that requires a bigger viewpoint — one that stretches across centuries even. When I saw that, it started making more sense.

"Tucker Hull. The founder of this whole clan. The one who left the Moravians to create his own version of religion — a sort of shadow Unitas Fratrum. Very secretive. You guys have gone to incredible lengths to remove as much mention of you as you could find. Hull never wanted anybody to know anything about him. Especially after he married Eve Hull. Especially after she taught him about witches and magic. Hull never wanted anybody to know that he used evil forces to gain wealth and to destroy those in his way. But, of course, you can't become as wealthy as the Hull family and leave no trace behind. And there were those pesky journals. Stan's was out there somewhere, and you needed to get it into your possession. The Hull journal, however — I'm guessing that every patriarch in this family has continued writing in that one. It's the only real record of your organization and your crimes."

Modesto slouched as his face took on a queasy appearance.

Max continued, "So what about those POWs? Stan said he noticed an odd look of recognition between one of them and Hull. That's why he tried the blackmail route. And he was right. There was recognition. The POW was a German named Günther Scholz. Now the Moravians, the branch that led to Tucker Hull living in North Carolina, well they're the German Moravians. William Hull knew of the Schulz family name and when he learned that Günther was being brought over to help make cigarettes, he used his witch to set up a meeting with Günther. He had seven POWs sent to the Reynolds factory in Winston-Salem and arranged to have a tour of the factory the same day. They shared a look, but it told Hull all he needed to know. He had been noticed as more than just a good businessman. Günther saw the leader of the cult who perverted his religion. Of course, Hull couldn't just kill the man. Too much attention gets wrapped up in a murder. So, he used Stan to eliminate the possibility of being revealed. When Stan lost it, he tried to stop the whole thing, but the kidnappings had drawn too much attention. It was too late. That's why Hull couldn't get rid of Annabelle. If she had met up with an accident, the press would've really started digging. And protecting your little cult is everything. So, instead, he bought her off.

"But that was a long time ago, and I suspect William Hull is dead. The Hull in charge now is trying to get back to the world of anonymity that his family has cultured and enjoyed for so long. And that is what this is all about. Secrecy."

Modesto shook his head in disbelief, but his hard face told Max the strikes were hitting close to the heart. "This is absurd," Modesto said. "If the Hull Group wanted secrecy so badly, why on Earth would they hire you to come look into the Moravians? It makes no sense."

"Because you needed to find that journal, and you wanted to test how secure your secrets were. You figured that if I couldn't find out anything about Hull, then the average person not even looking, or maybe some gung-ho reporter, nobody like that would ever find out. And then even if I never found a single thing about Hull, you were planning on doing away with us. Let the witch practice a few spells, perhaps. Get rid of every thread that led to Hull. Isn't that right? No need to answer. For now, there is one question that still bothers me. Perhaps you'll help."

"To this ridiculous —"

"I just can't figure out why you had Stephen Bowman arrested. On the one hand, you were trying to ease my mind, keep me focused, but that's not enough. You could have killed him, gotten the journal, and made up any story you wanted to satisfy me. Why put him in jail?"

Anger, or perhaps burned pride, swept across Modesto like an unforeseen squall. "Kill you, kill him — you're awfully quick with murder, Mr. Porter. We, however, are not. We are not thugs. We are not miscreants. And we are certainly not criminals. We merely appreciate a deep level of privacy, and for that, we are willing to go to great lengths."

"Is that what the witchcraft is all about? Great lengths?"

"There was never the intention of killing Stephen Bowman," Modesto said, his fists clutched white. "I had him put in jail so you would not get hurt and so you would not find him. You just couldn't let it lie, though. You had to keep digging."

"It's my job."

"How smug you are now. I assure you that even if we don't kill people with the casualness you suggest, we do know ways to make you pay dearly for threatening us."

"I have no doubt."

This caused Modesto to pause. "Then why do this? You've been running around the city for over a day. You clearly know the kind of trouble you're in. What do you get out of it?"

"The only thing that ever matters — my freedom."

"Perhaps you don't understand the true depths of what is going on here."

"I do," Max said, taking one step further. "And now, I'm going to tell you exactly what will happen. First off, you and Mr. Hull are going to call off all threats against me, Sandra, and the Bowmans. You'll also stop the surveillance. Basically, you're going to back out of our lives and leave us in peace."

From the back corner, Drummond shouted, "Keep the office."

"This office stays with me," Max said.

"Rent free."

"No rent. Consider it part of my severance package. In exchange for all of this, I will see to it that Hull's journal is returned. Of course, a complete copy of the journal will remain in my possession. Should anything happen to me, Sandra, or the Bowmans, the contents of that journal will be made public, as well as the results of all my research."

Modesto tucked in his shirt, straightened his hair, and looked a shade whiter. "All of that would be acceptable, if I believed you actually had Mr. Hull's journal. However, you don't. Everything you've said has been nothing more than conjecture — well-researched conjecture, I grant you, but conjecture nonetheless."

"You might be mistaken," Max said, holding up a sheet of paper.

"What's that?" Modesto asked, a visible tremor rumbling across him.

"This would be the binding curse written into the back pages of Hull's journal. I'm afraid when I return the journal, this page will be missing."

Drummond zipped across the room. "You got it! I never

doubted you, ever. You're the best friend I could ever have."

"Again," Modesto said, "without seeing the actual journal, I find this all rather unconvincing."

"I'm convinced," Drummond laughed. "Destroy it. Please. Set me free."

Max removed a match from the matchbox. "I'm standing in the center of the binding circle. When I light this paper, the ghost of Detective Marshall Drummond will be released. I suspect when he finds out why he was cursed, he'll be quite displeased."

"Now you claim to know that as well?"

"You're damn right. Poor Drummond had stumbled too close, and Hull was ready to have him killed."

"I told you, we don't —"

"Yes, you do. See, I found the little bits of a paper trail you've all missed. I found the transfer orders for the POWs, the ones Hull forced to happen. Funny thing about them, though, seven POWs go but only six return. How can that be? This is before Stan Bowman. And then I saw it — Hull had Günther from the start. He just didn't know what to do with the man. Now, this next part is a lot of conjecture, but I think it'll probably be close to the truth. Hull had been sleeping with a young woman, a witch. She also had bedded Marshall Drummond. And together, she and Hull came up with an idea of what to do with his POW problem. He would have her put a binding curse on the POW, just to make sure his privacy was maintained. However, she never did one before, so they cursed Drummond as a test and a way to get rid of Hull's rival."

"Entirely false."

"You may think so. It doesn't really matter. If I were you, being the sole representative of Hull standing in this room, I wouldn't want to be around that angry ghost when he's released. Of course, since you don't believe this is the actual paper, you have nothing to fear."

When Max lit the match, Modesto inched backward toward the door.

"Let's make this simple," Max said. "I'm going to light this paper. If you remain here, I'll know you've chosen to turn down my demands, and I'll release the journal to the public. If you leave, that will be considered acceptance and we can continue our lives in this lovely city with our strained but healthy peace."

"Look at that bastard sweat. Give him a countdown. They hate that," Drummond said.

"I'll count to three," Max said, dangling the cursed paper just out of reach of the flame. "One ... two ..."

Modesto stormed out, slamming the door behind him.

"Three," Max said and let the paper burn. He set it in the circle and stepped back. In seconds, the fire consumed the sheet and there was an audible pop like an enormous light bulb burning out.

Sandra rushed over to Max. "You did great."

"Great?" Drummond said. "Look at me."

Max and Sandra could not find him. "Where are you?" Max asked.

"Behind you."

Floating outside the window, Drummond waved and did a gleeful spin. "Congratulations," Max said. "And thanks."

Drummond slid back into the office. "No, no. I'm the one thanking you. I can't believe you found the journal, and making a copy was a bright idea."

"I don't have a copy. I lied."

"You're kidding."

"No. When I told Bowman my plan, he refused to help me out. He thought it was too risky giving the journal back."

"But he gave you the cursed paper?"

"I threatened to tell Modesto everything about him. Of course, Modesto already knew but Bowman didn't know that."

Sandra frowned. "But Modesto thinks he's getting the journal. What happens when he doesn't get it?"

"He will get it. I'm going back to the jail tomorrow, and I'll tell Bowman what I did. He's got no choice. Either he copies the journal and returns the original to Hull, or his grandmother is in danger and he'll be dead before the end of the week. My only worry was that Modesto would press the issue before I worked out the details with Bowman."

"A good bluff, you rascal," Drummond said.

"Tomorrow, I won't be bluffing."

"I tell you, if I were a genie instead of a ghost, I'd gladly grant you a thousand wishes."

"Throwing in that bit about this office was enough. Now I've got a place to work that won't cost us anything."

"What work?" Sandra asked.

Max raised an eyebrow before he kissed her with a long, loving embrace.

Chapter 30

FOUR MONTHS HAD PASSED. Sitting behind his desk, Max still found the whole experience hard to believe. That first week had been the strangest.

He enjoyed a final visit with Annabelle Bowman in which, for once, she was pleased to see him. He told her the truth about her husband and how she no longer needed to fear Hull. She offered him a bit of vodka and said, "You're a silly boy. I don't fear Hull. There's nothing he could do to me anymore."

A few weeks later, he filed all the necessary papers to officially start his own business as a research consultant. "What exactly is that?" Sandra asked.

Max shrugged. "Whatever somebody wants me to look into, I guess." They shared a look, one that said she knew what he really wanted to call his new venture but could not do so legally — private investigator.

"Do you think there'll be enough work?" she asked.

"I don't know, but I'm tired of us living under other people's rules. It wasn't just Drummond's freedom we won. It's ours, too."

"Sounds like there's going to be a lot of work."

"Why do you say that?"

"Sounds to me," Sandra said with an impish grin, "you'll be needing a secretary, maybe even an assistant."

"Oh, well, now that you mention it — yup, I just might. Maybe a young, hot, buxom little secretary."

"That's the kind of gal Drummond would hire. You need somebody more sophisticated, more reliable, and more sexy."

"You have somebody in mind?"

Sandra playfully slapped his chest. "If you don't let me work with you, you'll sleep on this office couch for the rest of your life."

"How about we sleep on it together, my new assistant?"

The next day, Max left a single rose on Sandra's desk. For a moment, she stared at it and smiled. The silence was wonderful.

Work trickled in — two cases really. One was finding a lost dog, and the other dealt with an odd fellow who wanted help researching his family tree. Max's mother called every week, each time showing her great enthusiasm for his endeavor.

"I don't understand you. You were a bright kid. You could have been a lawyer or a doctor. Why are you doing this?"

"I'm happy. Isn't that enough?"

"But what do I tell the girls at the bridge club?"

"You could try the truth."

"Don't get smart with me, young man. I'm still your mother. Now, what about kids? How are you going to have kids when you have to struggle to make ends meet? I'm not one to butt in your life — you never really listened to me anyway — but you're ruining your life this way."

After Stephen Bowman delivered the journal, Max had not heard from Modesto. That was fine by him. In fact, he only harbored sadness for Drummond. About an hour after being freed, Drummond became difficult to see — even to Sandra. A little bit later, he had disappeared entirely. But Max hoped that Drummond was in a peaceful place, wherever spirits go.

"Wake up, Max," Drummond barked as he flew through the office walls, looking thicker than ever.

"Drummond? What are you doing here? Why aren't you plucking harps or dancing on clouds or something?"

"It was boring. I can't even begin to tell you how boring. Besides, I kept peeking in here and I could see you needed my help. You've had two cases and you botched them both."

"I solved them."

"Well, yeah, but you could've billed them for far more money and used them to leverage out a few more gigs. You've gotta learn about per diem, kiddo."

"You came all the way back here to tell me that?"

Drummond gazed at the second desk in the office. "Well, well, you've got the missus with you, huh? Dangerous move."

"I thought you said you were watching me. Why didn't you know Sandra was here until now?"

"Hey, I can't be expected to take care of all the details. That's your job. I'm the guy who steers this ship in the right direction which it ain't going in at the moment. That's why I came back. You need me."

"Hold on. Stop. You are not a partner in this."

"Sure I am. This is my office."

"It's mine, now."

"Thanks to me."

"You're dead, for crying out loud. You're not supposed to be here."

Drummond sat in Sandra's seat and spun it around. "I know, I know, but really that's a small detail, and one you don't have to worry anything about. They're not going to miss me up there anyway. I think most of them think it was a mistake in the first place. Besides, I'm valuable to you."

"You are?"

"I'm going to bring you clients."

"You are?"

"Got one lined up already."

"A client?"

"Sure. The guy's name is Barney. He made this will, but his wife — who if you ask me may have poisoned the guy, though she's quite a looker — well, she's using the old will, the one that gives her all of his estate. So, he wants you —"

Max raised a hand. "Barney's dead?"

"Of course. There's a whole slew of ghosts who could make great use of a guy like you. And they'll pay anything. They don't need money anymore."

Max opened his mouth, ready to send Drummond back from where he came. Yes, the bills were stacking up. Yes, he was glad to see his old friend. And yes, the two cases he had were not very interesting because of their mundane nature. But he pointed a finger at Drummond and said, "Look —"

"Sounds like a great idea," Sandra said from the doorway. "Just promise us we won't be dealing with ex-girlfriend witches again, okay?"

"Done," Drummond said.

Both of them looked to Max who shook his head. He opened his mouth, ready to list the infinite reasons this was a bad idea, but said nothing. He glanced at Sandra, smiled, and saw in her eyes something he always trusted whenever he saw it. He just knew she was right.

Afterword

For those of you wondering about the historical facts, I don't want to add pages and pages of non-fiction here, so I encourage you to do some research of your own. I will say that this story grew out of learning about the very real POW camps we had in North Carolina. That really happened.

Also, for those of you wanting to drive around Winston-Salem to see the various places mentioned, I promise you that you'll never find Max's office. The only thing that sits across the street from the YMCA is a parking lot. Many other locations do exist, though I sometimes took liberties with the details. This is fiction, after all.

About the Author

Stuart Jaffe is the author of *The Malja Chronicles*, *After The Crash*, and *10 Bits of My Brain*, as well as numerous short stories appearing in magazines and anthologies. He is the co-host of The Eclectic Review — a podcast about science, art, and well, everything. For those who keep count, the latest animal listing is as follows: five cats, one albino corn snake, one Brazilian black tarantula, three aquatic turtles, one tortoise, assorted fish, two lop-eared rabbits, eight chickens, and a horse. Thankfully, the chickens and the horse do not live inside the house.

For more information visit www.stuartjaffe.com

MAX PORTER RETURNS IN

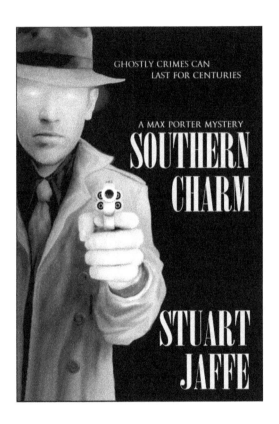

GHOSTLY CRIMES CAN
LAST FOR CENTURIES

A MAX PORTER MYSTERY

SOUTHERN CHARM

STUART
JAFFE

AVAILABLE NOW!

CPSIA information can be obtained
at www.ICGtesting.com
Printed in the USA
LVHW012045060120
642661LV00007B/1369